Hidden Eyes

Hidden Eyes

Based on a true story by Spiritualist medium

Suzanne Gill

Published by Createspace com

© Copyright Suzanne Gill 2016

HIDDEN EYES

All rights reserved.

The right of Suzanne Gill to be identified as the author of this work has been asserted in accordance with the Copyright, Designs, and Patents Act 1988.

No part of this publication may be reproduced, stored in a retrieval system, or transmitted, in any form or by any means, electronic, mechanical, photocopying, recording, or otherwise, nor translated into a machine language, without the written permission of the publisher.

Condition of sale

This book is sold subject to the condition that it shall not, by way of trade or otherwise, be lent, re-sold, hired out or otherwise circulated in any form of binding or cover other than that in which it is published and without a similar condition including this condition being imposed on the subsequent purchaser.

ISBN 978-1-530-60695-5

Book formatted by www. bookformatting. co. uk.

Contents

August 2004	Sam's Story	1
Suzanne's Story		9
15th September	Unintentional War	11
17th September	Dog Soldier	37
18th September	Before the storm	42
18th September	Team Building	47
18th September	Salt and Circles	51
18th September	Reaching Out	57
20th September	Sadness Grows	63
20th September	Intimidation	70
21st September	A Visit from The Canadians	88
22nd September	Breaking News	108
23rd September	Second Opinion	126
23rd September	Lifting The Blindfold	139

Acknowledgements

I would like to dedicate Hidden Eyes to my beautiful daughter Francesca. For all her hard work co-writing my story and support throughout the most traumatic experiences of my life.

HIDDEN EYES was written from our hearts!

Francesca, you are my inspiration and the best friend anyone can ever ask for in life. Thank you for being there through the good times and the bad. You are my hero xx

Thank you also to Yvonne McDonagh and Sandra Brannigan for proof reading my story xx

And finally to my manager Mike Trewhella, for turning my story into the book you will now read.

Suzanne Gill

March 2016

Foreword by Suzanne

It has taken me until now to be able to put into words what I have carried in my heart and head for so long.

Sometimes it feels like it happened only yesterday.

The events you are going to read about, changed me physically and mentally. They wrecked my relationship and I found it hard to resume a normal life afterwards. I have never completely got over my experiences and I still carry a burden to this very day.

My name is Suzanne, and I have been a medium since the age of sixteen. At the time I write of, I was twenty-nine and in a good relationship with my partner Mark who I'd known for about three years.

We had two lovely children, my daughter Francesca aged seven, and son Alex fifteen months old. We lived on a small but pleasant housing estate on the northern outskirts of Sunderland.

I was making a living by giving psychic readings on a one to one basis or attending house parties to provide group readings. I knew quite a few of the other readers in the area and we often met up with each other at the various 'Psychic Fairs' occurring around the North East.

One of the organisers of these Psychic Fairs was a guy named John. He'd known me for quite a while and gave me bookings at some of his events. He is the link to the place that has caused me so much pain and trouble.

It was John who introduced me to the Wheatsheaf Public House in West Boldon, South Tyneside, an introduction I wish now, I'd turned down. However, what's done is done and no matter what I do, I'll never be able to turn the clock back.

I will let Sam, the deputy manager of the pub begin this story by giving you an insight into what triggered the series of events I was drawn into. I will then take over and tell you my side of the story which includes scenes that I will carry for the rest of my life.

Suzanne Gill
March 2016

August 2004
Sam's Story

'Morning!' I greeted cheerily, trying to mask my anxiousness. 'Morning Sam, how are you?' Mary the cleaner asked with a wry smile. 'I'm fine, bloody knackered after all these goings on,' I laughed, I always tried to brush off the uneasiness I felt in the bar. I dreaded each shift as something always happened on a day to day basis in here, from bangs to pints being tipped over, it was getting worse lately. 'I know, it's scary isn't it? Especially being here on my own cleaning, it really gives me the shivers' she replied as she cleaned the tables, all ready for another day.

I never knew what to expect anymore, it was so surreal. I had never experienced anything like this before. The only reason I stayed on at this place was because jobs were tight and I really needed to keep my position as deputy manager of the Wheatsheaf, a public house in the little village of West Boldon, Tyne & Wear.

I took off my jacket and put my handbag away behind the bar, it was so warm as you'd expect of an August morning, hopefully, it would stay warm for a while longer before the autumn set in. I looked around and saw a note from Phil, the pub manager, asking me to check on the beer kegs. Instantly a wave of fear washed over me, as I realized

I would have to go down to the cellar. I hated going down there as I always felt I was being watched as if someone or something didn't want me to be there. 'Mary can you do me a favour?' I asked. 'Of course love,' she replied, setting down her rag and tin of polish on the bar. 'Can you come to the cellar with me? I'm too scared to go by myself.' Her face went pale. I knew from what I'd heard on the grapevine Mary experienced a few strange things happen down there as well. A number of rumours were circulating about strange happenings in the pub and I'd had first-hand experience of some of them. I brought to mind an incident that had occurred only a few weeks previously. I'd spent all afternoon making vodka jelly for the happy hour the next night. I put the jelly trays into the fridge to set. They were perfect in their clear glass bowls. I was quite pleased with the result.

The next morning on returning to work I went to the fridge for the jellies. On opening the door I was stunned to a see the imprint of a small child's hand on one of the jellies. I screamed so loud that two of the barmen, Chris and Tony came running to see what was up. I showed them the hand print. I was shaking.

All the staff knew that the fridge was always kept locked. I shook my head and tried to let the memory fade before going down into the cellar.

It was so eerie down there and from Mary's expression, I could see she was reluctant to join me. The memory of the jelly incident was still fresh in my mind as I grabbed the cellar keys from behind the bar. 'Come on, let's get it over with!' I said making my way to the cellar entrance.

Mary followed me timidly down the stairs, her head turning from side to side as if she would see something lurking in a dark corner. I pulled at the big wooden door, it was so heavy. I managed to open it just enough for us both to squeeze through. I walked over to the kegs and checked them all, making notes of which ones needed to be replaced.

'I don't like it in here Sam. I feel as though someone is watching me,' Mary whispered. I turned to look at her. 'I won't be long, just another couple of minutes.' I smiled trying to shake the overbearing feeling of being observed. I quickly checked the remaining kegs and we exited the cellar as fast as we could, almost running up the stairs.

The cellar had sent shivers up both our spines. 'Thank God that's over and done with,' Mary exclaimed. I settled into my normal routine and forgot about the cellar.

It was a quiet day and as usual, only a few regulars sat quietly watching the racing on the TV, sipping their pints in companionable silence. Chris and Phil joined me in the bar. 'Hi, guys!' I smiled.

'Hey Sam, you won't believe what happened to us last night,' Chris blurted out while Phil nodded from behind. 'Why? What happened?' I asked, leaning closer to them.

'Well... we were walking upstairs, just going to double check everything was shut. We didn't even get to top of the landing when something tried to push us down the stairs!' I gasped, 'Are you serious?' My heart was racing with fear. 'Yeah, but that's not all, we heard a man laughing while we were being forced back downstairs. It's getting worse in here.'

I couldn't believe what I was hearing, it seemed things were definitely taking a turn for the worst regarding all the paranormal stuff going on.

'This needs to stop,' I sighed, grabbing a cloth and wiping the already immaculate bar surface, trying to do something to occupy myself. Business had become slow and it was largely down to the rumours that had spread about the terrifying happenings.

'Why don't we tell these ghosts or whatever they are to stop?' Phil murmured, as he pulled out a barstool and sat down in front of me.

'What makes you think they'll listen?' I laughed sarcastically, whatever was traipsing around didn't feel friendly. Telling it off could make matters worse.

'They'll listen if we have this.' He reached into the bag on his shoulder and pulled out a pile of laminated letters.

'How will that make them listen?' I asked, shuffling through the pile of cards showing alphabetical letters. Coming to a stop on one card that said 'yes', it then dawned on me that he wanted to make a Ouija board. I'd never had much experience with them, but I'd watched many horror films, and I knew how they worked. Denise, my friend, had told me about one of her relatives going crazy after using one. To say I was dubious was an understatement. A shiver crawled up my spine. I knew instantly that this was a very bad idea, probably the worst one Phil has ever had.

'It's for a Ouija board,' Phil stated, as Chris took the laminated letters from my hand and began to flip through them just as I had. 'We can do it tonight. Let's find out what on earth is banging about and hopefully ask it to leave,' he smiled looking as though he thought this was the best plan in the world, it was far from it.

'I don't think this is a good idea', I finally voiced, 'Isn't it dangerous?' I looked at Phil and he gave me a reassuring smile as if butter wouldn't melt.

'It will be fine, we just need to ask it to stop scaring people, whoever it is,' I nodded. I was curious to know who was banging around and giving the pub such a poor reputation. As they say; *curiosity killed the cat.* I knew stupidly, that my curiosity always got the better of me.

'Okay then, let's do it,' I smiled sheepishly, earning a

nod from Chris and Phil who were both unnaturally excited about the whole thing.

'We will do it after we lock up, just in here' said Phil 'We'll sit at one of the tables,' Chris chirped in. I just nodded and tried to put the uneasy feeling this brought, to the back of my mind.

After our little group chat in the afternoon, the day flew by. I couldn't stop the sick churning in the pit of my stomach, my gut feeling was to keep away from the Ouija board. But I knew I couldn't do that, I was too intrigued to know who was haunting this place. Even admitting the pub was haunted seemed to scare me. I spent the majority of my week here, and I didn't want to make whoever it was angry or more active.

As the time to lock up approached and I'd rang the bell for last orders. I was making myself nervous thinking of all the things that potentially could go wrong. Horrible scenarios were playing over and over in my head, as I tried to join in on Phil's conversation with Chris.

'It's almost time,' Phil stated, as he checked his watch. 'Half past eleven, should I get everything set up?' I mutely nodded as he took the protective glass sheet off the table and began to place the letters on the wooden surface. Whilst all the cards were laid out and covered with the glass sheet, I made sure the main doors to the pub were locked. Phil and Chris were already at the table waiting for me to join them. I took a deep breath and walked through the bar into the lounge, taking the seat next to Chris and opposite Phil. Tony had joined us, sitting just outside of our little circle. He had reluctantly agreed to take some notes but didn't want any further involvement.

'Are we ready?' Phil asked. We all nodded. I looked down at the table where the letters were placed in a semicircle with yes and no in the middle. Phil took a glass from under his seat, just a normal whisky tumbler, nothing too big or heavy. He placed it on the glass sheet and the three of us placed our index fingers on the glass.

'Is anyone here with us?' Phil asked. Nothing ... just the quiet hum of the fridges filled the room.

'Ask again,' Chris said, 'only louder.' Phil took a deep breath before repeating the phrase, much louder this time. I quickly looked around the room. The thought of seeing someone or something terrified me. Nothing had changed. A still silence enveloped us. Suddenly the glass jerked to one side.

'Very funny,' I muttered. 'Who moved that?' I looked accusingly at Chris and Phil. They just shook their heads; they were equally shocked that the glass had actually moved.

I whispered 'Is anyone here with us?' The glass shot to *'yes'*, I instantly removed my fingers.

'No Sam, don't take your fingers off!' Phil said abruptly, and I quickly returned them, hearing the sternness in his voice.

'What is your name?' Chris asked. The glass began to slowly move, picking up some momentum as it finished spelling the word 'Joseph.' At least, there was a name, I thought to myself. It made the spirit seem more human rather than a nameless entity causing havoc. 'Are you the one who scares people and knocks glasses off the tables?' The glass shot to the word 'yes', and for a faint second, I could swear I heard a little laugh from behind me. The room had grown darker. It was almost pitch black as if something was blocking out the faint light from the streetlights outside.

'Why do you scare people?' I asked quietly. The glass moved frantically around the table. We read out each letter and Tony wrote the following message down.

'This is my pub, they are getting in my way,' said Tony, as he read out what he had written.

'You are dead!!' Phil shouted, overcome by a rage the like of which I had never seen in him before. 'This is my pub now; you need to get out!!' As soon as he had finished that sentence, an almighty bang against the fire door resonated around the room.

'Was that him?' I asked, feeling the fear in my bones. 'Yes.' The glass moved faster, rotating around the table, spelling out another sentence. It was difficult to keep up with the glass as it moved over the cards. My arms began to ache.

The next message was, 'Get out or I'll kill you all!!'. I didn't like the sound of that. My fingers were shaking on the glass and I could feel tears streaming down my face.

'I think that's enough for tonight,' Phil said, obviously as scared as I was. I looked at Chris, he had a blank face. I could almost see the gears turning in his head as he tried to comprehend what had just happened. I quickly took my fingers off the glass relieved that I didn't have to touch it anymore.

Just as we were about to get up, the glass moved ever so slightly. I looked at Phil, he just raised his eyebrows and returned one finger to the glass. I sighed, placing both of my index fingers on the top the glass. It slowly started to move. It was hard to explain but it felt like someone different was moving it this time.

The movements of the glass spelled out, 'Help me please!'. We heard a child's cry echo through the room. The glass moved again spelling out, 'Help me' continuously, then it suddenly paused before touching the letters that spelled, 'Help me Suzanne.' The glass became still. We heard a child's footsteps running up the stairs.

I was shocked. It hit me like a bolt of lightening. The

incident with the vodka jelly! I knew who had placed their tiny hand onto the jelly in the fridge.

'Oh God!' I cried. 'We have to save her'.

Phil and Chris looked at me, then to Tony. 'How do you know it's a girl?' they asked in unison. I just shook my head.

'I just know in my heart it's a little girl.' I wiped away my tears.

'I think we should try and connect with the child again soon,' Chris said quietly. We all nodded in agreement.

There was one thing playing on my mind... who the hell was Suzanne?

Suzanne's Story

15th September
Unintentional War

Resting on my cosy leather armchair, I was enjoying five minutes' peace and quiet. It is the first chance I had to do so since opening my eyes that morning. All I had done was rush around. Everything I did seemed to be a challenge, I hated feeling unorganised. I was worn out by this time every day, the school run was hectic, and my son Alex was finally asleep in his pushchair after a morning of tantrums because he couldn't go with his Dad Mark, who had a doctor's appointment.

'Thank God' I thought, now I can rest. I glanced at the clock on the top of the mantelpiece, it was 12:45 pm. Sinking my exhausted body deeper into the armchair, I allowed my mind to slowly drift off.

I thought about the past few months, about how my new challenge was starting to unfold. For the first time in years, I could see my life mapped out in front of me. Since May, I felt my career had slowly begun to grow. I was building up some recognition in the psychic circuits, my dream of becoming a respected spiritualist medium was turning into a reality. I settled down, let myself relax and began daydreaming.

Looking out of the living room window, I watched the clouds floating by. It was moments like this I loved, just to sit and reflect on my future ahead. My relaxed state was interrupted by my mobile phone ringing in my handbag. Quickly I jumped up and rummaged around until I finally found it. Looking at my mobile, I realised it was a number I didn't recognise. I quietly left the living room and went into the dining room, trying not to disturb Alex who was sound asleep in his pushchair. 'Hello.' I whispered down the phone, as I pulled up a chair from my dining table and sat down. I placed my elbow on the shiny polished surface and began rubbing at some little bits of dust I'd missed after tidying up less than an hour ago.

'Hi,' said a man's voice, 'is this Suzanne?'

'Yes,' I replied with a hesitant tone.

'Hi Suzanne, it's John.'

Then it suddenly dawned on me who the man's voice belonged to, it was the organiser for the psychic fair I was supposed to attend later that evening.

'Oh Hi John, how are you?'

'I am fine,' he said, but I could sense his manner said otherwise, very different from his usual laid back self. It didn't take a spiritualist medium to pick up on the fact that he was really stressed.

'I am checking to see if you're okay for the charity night at the Wheatsheaf pub tonight?'.

'Oh yes,' I answered, rolling my eyes, trying hard to think up an excuse to say that I wouldn't be attending.

'Don't let me down Suzanne,' came his firm voice on the end of the line.

'No, I won't let you down,' I said reassuring him I was attending but mentally kicking myself for committing to this charity night in the first place. 'I wouldn't let you down, John.' He sounded exhausted. 'I am fed up with other psychics on the circuit cancelling for this charity night at the last minute. I have organised this night for all of us to give back some goodness and gratitude to the community.' I could relate to what he was saying.

'Charity is good for the soul,' I commented. He let out a laugh and agreed. The conversation continued in a pleasant light-hearted manner. I had been working for John the past two months. He was one of the biggest organisers of psychic fairs in the North East. John had helped me establish myself by introducing me to his events. It was only fair to support his charity night in return for him taking me under his wing. As the conversation was drawing to a close I could hear the tone of his voice had softened towards me.

'Right,' he said. 'Do you know where you are going?'

'Yes, I have the directions written down in my diary,' I said, as I thumbed through the worn red book. I found the scribbled map I had jotted down days previously.

'Well... I will see you tonight at 6 pm.'

'Oh no John,' I interrupted. 'Can I make it for 7 pm, as I have to collect my daughter from school?'

'Oh alright... Don't let me down Suzanne!' he repeated.

'I won't, I have promised I will be there and I am not the type to go back on my word,' I replied.

As we ended the call I rubbed my eyes and thought to myself, another night away from the kids was the last thing I needed. Over the last few months, I had been working a lot of late nights. I was concerned this was becoming a normality for me and my family. *Oh, it's only one night,* I thought to myself, as I looked forward to the coming weekend. Three days off promised lots of quality time for me to spend with my family. I was reluctant to refuse any work that came my way as I didn't want to tarnish my reputation... and as the old saying goes; *'don't look a gift horse in the mouth'.*

Walking back from my dining room, and into the

kitchen, I picked up the kettle and began to fill it with water. I turned around and saw a message on the family notice board highlighted in bold red writing, *Mum its shopping day*. Underneath the red writing was a list of items needed for the house. Francesca my daughter, was good at keeping me organised.

'Oh God,' I said out loud while running my fingers through my hair, trying to release the tension, 'It's shopping day.' I wasn't looking forward to the next two hours of shopping that lay ahead. I made a cup of tea and sat down with distressing images filling my head. Alex in a shopping centre was not a good combination.

Alex was only one-year-old and already clued up on throwing a temper tantrum in the aisles, reaching out to pick up any object that looked colourful. and when he didn't get what he wanted, the next '*Let's scream the shop down*' phase began. Oh, the joys!! Shopping days were rapidly becoming a nightmare. The only way I could describe a shopping day is being a contestant on supermarket sweep, dashing around the aisles at a great speed, packing everything I needed into the trolley and rushing to the checkout. My main aim was to get in and out of there as quickly as humanly possible.

After a hectic couple of hours shopping with Mark and collecting Francesca from school, there wasn't much time left to relax before leaving for work. When we got home I spent some time watching TV with the kids but too soon the clock showed 6 pm.

I picked up my work bag. It was full of Native American ornaments, candles and a few bits and pieces I like to place on my table when I read for the public. These items make me feel more connected with my spirit guides and help me channel messages from loved ones during readings.

15TH SEPTEMBER UNINTENTIONAL WAR

I gave the kids a kiss and stepped out of the front door, the cold air hit my lungs. *I hate being cold*, I thought. I ran to my car parked opposite the house and after placing my bag in the boot I climbed into the front seat. Before I started the engine I opened up my diary and looked at the date, it was the 15th of September.

Right, I thought to myself as I rolled my index finger down the page, I was trying to visualise the right road to go on and decided to search through my A to Z. I had estimated a time in my head of about thirty minutes for the drive. I started the car and drove out of the estate picturing street names as I ticked them off the list in my head; it was my own form of navigating.

I was approaching a roundabout. The signpost showed South Shields to the right but underneath was a little white sign marked Boldon to the left. This road took me past Sunderland Dog Stadium. A little further down the road, I entered the village of East Boldon. I didn't recognise this place at all. Old Victorian houses on either side, making me feel like I had stepped back in time. I eventually arrived at a set of traffic lights. When the lights changed to green I moved off and saw to my right, the street I was looking for, St. Nicholas Road. Oh, Fab! It wasn't difficult to find at all. There was a small car park at the rear of the pub. I parked, switched off the engine and sat for a couple of minutes to compose myself.

I was feeling some discomfort in my stomach, which had started as soon as I saw the building. Thinking I must have eaten something that didn't agree with me, I placed my hand on my abdomen to find a sore spot, but there didn't seem to be anything wrong. I had a feeling of apprehension that usually only occurred when someone close to me was in trouble. *Oh God!* I thought, *I hope my family are okay*. My parents were visiting my brother in

Spain and my younger brother lived in China. Normally when a feeling comes on as quick as this, it's a warning for me to be prepared that fate had something in store for me. I tried to ignore the feeling and glanced at my reflection in the rear view mirror checking my mascara was in place. Making a good impression was important to me. Checking the time on the dashboard, 6:50 pm, *right*, I thought to myself, *let's get this night over with. I can go home and wind down with Mark.*

As I stepped out of the car, I noticed in front of me a white wall running along the back of the car park. Glancing around I could see some lights on the back of the building were lit up, especially near the fire exit door behind me. I looked to the right and could make out a sitting area with decking and a couple of benches. Walking round towards the boot of my car I had this awful dread in my heart. I couldn't shake off the way I was feeling. I lifted the boot and grabbed my work bag. I turned to see some trees behind the wall situated at the side of the pub. I walked towards an entrance when I was suddenly startled by a gentle stroking on one side of my face. I looked down to see a tiny feather falling to the ground. It had touched my face and was floating towards my feet. I placed a hand beneath to catch it. It lay gently in the palm of my hand glistening in the light. It comprised of lovely colours and I was fascinated that something so small and beautiful could radiate so much light. This feeling sent a shiver down my spine. I placed the feather in my pocket for safe keeping. I turned to notice a window above the side door. There was a dim light shining through the dirty pane. I was at a loss as to why I felt so drawn yet so repelled by this strange building. Briefly ever so briefly, a small figure appeared at the window. I saw a little girl looking down at me. There was something odd about her appearance. She seemed almost transparent. A split second later she was gone. I stood in the middle of the car park astonished at what I had just witnessed.

After a moment, I collected my thoughts and entered the pub. The place was packed with people queuing up for readings. *Oh my God*! I thought to myself, *this is going to be a fun filled night*! I couldn't hear myself think. It was like walking into a wall of sound. I searched for the organizer in the crowd, pushing my way through the throng of bodies. Every step I took, made my annoyance grow. I felt suffocated. There were far too many people in this one room. Pushing my way towards the bar, I knew I didn't want to be in this pub a moment longer than necessary.

Whilst standing at the bar, I noticed a woman carrying a clipboard, moving through the crowd. She had short black hair, slim build and her skin was a lovely golden brown colour. I waved for her to come over to me. The queues at the bar were getting longer. The more time I spent in this pub, the more irritated I felt.

The lady with a clipboard came walking towards me. 'Hi, I am Sam, the deputy manager of the Wheatsheaf,' she said.

'Hi Sam' I replied, feeling relaxed as we shook hands. 'It's busy tonight'.

'Oh yes,' she replied as she flicked through some papers on her clipboard. 'You must be one of John's Psychics?' she asked.

'Yes,' I replied, 'Hi, I'm Suzanne, sorry I'm a bit late.'

She hesitated and a look came over her face that I couldn't quite interpret. After a few moments, she seemed to gain some composure and said. 'I am over the moon you've come along, here is a list of people you are reading for. There should be fifteen names on the sheet. Each one will have a ticket that they hand to you. Each customer expects about a fifteen-minute reading'

'Okay,' I said. I could see she was trying to keep the night as organised as possible.

I have a space for you in the corner,' she pointed towards a little table situated next to a big bay window that looked out onto the main road. A wooden screen beside the table provided a little privacy. 'Would you like me to bring a drink over for you,' She asked kindly. 'Yes, a soft drink would be nice.' I replied and we exchanged smiles. I grabbed my bag and headed to the corner. I entered a part of the bar that was sectioned off from the rest of the room, it was a little less crowded and I could see some familiar faces of other readers who also worked on the circuit. I didn't want to disturb them as I could see they were very busy working.

Sam had taken a little of the tension away because she was such a lovely chatty person who really made me feel welcome. At the table, I began the regular routine I always carried out before I started reading. First spreading my tablecloth then carefully laying out my Native American pictures and ornaments. Finally, I placed a small candle in the centre of the table. This helps to bring my guides through to me. I had a feeling I was going to need all the support I could get. I sat and closed my eyes trying to put myself into a state of spiritual communication but all the laughter and voices in the background made it difficult. Another psychic sitting on the table near to me was also finding it hard to work in such a noisy place.

My heart sank when I saw the long line of customers waiting for me to start the readings. I lit the candle and asked my guides to give me protection, mainly because I just couldn't shake off the feeling of dread I was carrying.

The first person on my list was a lady who appeared to be in her sixties. After taking her ticket we sat together and the reading began. At the end of the reading, the chair opposite me was quickly filled. Time passed quickly and the chair in front of me didn't stay empty for very long.

I could see the names on the list were becoming less and less. I sent out a message to my guides, thanking them for their love and support. *I can see a light at the end of tonight's tunnel of mayhem*, I thought to myself. Soon I was down to the ninth person on my list. She walked away tearful, but happy at getting a message from her mum in the spirit world. It was time for a break, I thanked my guides for all their help. Glancing at the time and saw it was 9:30 pm. *Oh great*, I thought. *I have an hour left before I can leave this madness behind me.* I stood up and moved away from the table. Sam was behind the bar serving drinks. She spotted me in the crowd and beckoned me over. Pushing my way through the crowd I slowly made my way to the bar.

Sam handed me a drink of coke and we began to strike up a conversation, the major topic being the charity night. Sam seemed very excited about it. I felt really at ease talking to her. She told me the event had raised an estimated sum of about £1000 for their chosen charity.

'Wow!' I said, 'that's really good news.' We both smiled at each other and the thought ran through my mind that the money raised would change peoples' lives for the better. I asked where the lady's toilets were and she directed me towards some stairs at the far end of the room. 'It's the first door at the top of the corridor,' she replied. There were many rows of dirty pint glasses lined up along the bar. 'Poor Sam' I thought, as I headed off towards the stairs.

Standing on the first step, I looked up the stairs to the window at the top of the landing. I could make out red curtains and netting but the lights were dim and it was hard to see details. I reached the top of the stairs and was turning to my left when, from the corner of my eye, I saw a blue light suddenly appear. My whole body just stopped moving. My feet were firmly stuck to the landing floor. Some kind of powerful force was pinning me down. I felt a presence close by. An aching pain struck me like an electric shock, making my stomach churn. The light moved in front of me. My heart was racing. From within the light, an image of a small frail young girl aged about of six with long golden blonde hair partly covering her thin face appeared before me. She was wearing a dull white and grey dress, with a faded pink pinafore layered on top. Little boots on her feet reminded me of the Victorian era. A date came into my mind, 1906, then a name, Suzanne. *But how can this be? That's my name! She couldn't possibly have the same name as me.* I put my hand over my mouth stifling a scream that was wanting to escape from my throat. I heard a series of loud bangs close by. Men and women were shouting, and chaos seemed all around me. The little girl's small face wore a mask of terror, she was begging me to help her. Her feeble little voice calling, 'Help Me!'. I couldn't tear my eyes away from her. That pleading look in her sad blue eyes touched my very soul. Time was standing still. Seconds felt like minutes. In the blink of an eye, she was running away from me, her footsteps sounding like the tap of metal on wood instead of the carpet that was actually there. A few seconds later the force that held me seemed to lift and my immediate reaction was to follow her. I headed along a short corridor towards a door signed 'Ladies toilets.' My heart was beating like a drum as I slowly opened the door, and entered. There was no sign of the little girl.

I couldn't get my head around what I had just seen out there in the corridor. Leaning against the wall I closed my eyes, taking deep breaths. A heavy feeling of sadness filled the room. All I wanted to do was cry. Fighting back the tears I opened my eyes and placed my bag on the floor letting out a sigh. I stood back up to face my own reflection in the mirror above the wash basin. I looked tired and there were dark bags under my eyes. My hair was a mess. I didn't have a brush or comb so I tidied it up by running my fingers through it. Every nerve ending was still on edge after the little girl incident and my head ached as I tried to make sense of it all. Whilst standing in front of the mirror for a minute or two to compose myself, another wave of fear came over me, but this time, it was much stronger. As I looked into the mirror I saw flashes of blue and white light behind me. The burgundy red colour of the toilets had been replaced with a small flowered and cream patterned wallpaper.

I spun around to see I was standing in a bedroom yet I knew I hadn't moved from the spot. The horizontal mirror had been replaced with a window and I could see daylight streaming in from outside. A netting and heavy cream curtains were partly covering the window. A small metal framed bed sat at the far left of the room. Some dolls were arranged upon a dresser to the right. Looking down, the floor had also changed. Only a small rug beside the bed offered any form of luxury from the old wooden floorboards. The room had a kind of a musty smell and left a stale taste in my mouth.

Faintly at first then becoming louder, I heard that same sad little voice pleading. 'Help Me... please.'

'I will help, what do you want me to do?' I asked desperately. Then she appeared again. Running through the door panting, as if being chased, she headed for the dresser, pulled open a drawer and took out a battered old tin box decorated with Victorian houses and a man riding a penny-farthing painted on the lid. After placing it on the floor the little girl tried to prize it open the tin with thin fumbling fingers. I felt that tears were streaming down from her face, although I could only see the back of her head.

I noticed bruises on her wrists and I started to cry, thinking about what could have happened to her. When the lid came off I could see the tin held photos and a few other small trinkets. She quickly pulled out of the tiny pocket in her grey dress, a silver locket with a thin chain. Both locket and chain were put safely into the tin. I could hear screams coming from the next room. Women crying and men shouting. Footsteps sounded in the corridor outside the room.

'Oh my God no! You can't touch her', I thought, *'leave her alone'*. I couldn't take my eyes off her. It was as if I was sharing the terrible memories in her life. The little girl seemed trapped and tormented by her past as if there was no relief from the pain that was haunting her soul. The noises and commotion continued, angry voices coming down the corridor, the screams getting louder. Tension in the room began to feel unbearable. I could see this poor little soul trying to find a hiding place in the room, and sensed she didn't have much time before she met her greatest nightmare.

The temperature in the room plunged and my body went into shock. I was powerless to save this little girl from her fate. This poor child cornered like an animal with no escape. She kept her head bowed looking at the floor. 'Help me, he is coming for me!' she cried.

I shouted back, 'Who is coming for you?'... Her voice started to fade.

'Help me please...' she whimpered.

Suddenly a bright light shone in through the window, momentarily blinding me and causing the bedroom to fade from my view. When my vision returned the bedroom was no more. Once again I stood in the Ladies toilets beside the washbasin looking into the mirror. I saw my haunted reflection looking back at me. I was struggling to take in the vivid scenes I had just witnessed. Tears were running down my face. Watching what may have been the last few moments of that child's life had left me devastated.

A surge of frustration came over me. *Come on Suzanne keep it together*, I tried to reassure myself, *you have less than an hour to go before you finish tonight's readings*. Leaving the toilets and making my way back down the stairs, I had a strong urge to grab my bag and run out of the pub and never return.

With reluctance to sit back down at my table, I glanced at my list to read the remaining names noticing there had been more names added to the list while I had been on my break! I had no other choice but to switch off my thoughts and concentrate on the next hour.

The event finally drew to a close, the bar slowly emptied and I glanced at my watch, 10:45 pm I looked around to see that some of the other clairvoyants had left by then. They'd given up with the endless list of names and walked out of the pub. There was only a handful of us left. I managed to briefly chat with one of them. She mentioned that it was her last ever charity night.

'It's been hell working in this pub tonight, surrounded by all this mayhem,' she said. I agreed with her, thinking of all the issues that had taken place here throughout the evening. Mediums like to work in quiet peaceful surroundings. 'I am complaining to John for the lack of organization and did you notice he was nowhere to be seen all night, not even a hello or a welcome?' she whispered, her face red with anger as she picked up her belongings, packing them into her bag. I suggested having a drink and a chat with me... 'Oh,' she said. 'I wish I could... but I have to drive an hour down the road and I am not keen on stopping in this pub for a second longer than I have to. It has a bad feel about it.'

'I understand, we'll catch up again some other time,' I replied. She gave me a hug picked up her bag and left.

My eyes were drawn to the stairs leading to the landing. Recalling the things that had just occurred there made me want to know more about that frightened child. *Maybe the staff could cast more light on things.* I thought.

I packed up my things and strolled over to Sam. She was standing at the end of the bar talking to a small group of men. She noticed me standing there and came over. 'You and your friends have been great tonight everyone is happy with their readings ... from you especially,' she said.

'Thank you,' I replied smiling. I told her that the night could have gone a lot better if there had been fewer present.

'Oh I know,' she said, 'it's been hard work for all of us tonight.' We made our way to the lounge bar, and Sam pulled up a tall stool, patting the top she said, 'Here, why don't you sit down and I'll get you a drink, what would you like?'

I rested my body on the stool, 'A coke would be great.' I replied. She quickly returned and placed my order in front of me. 'Here you go,' she said. We settled down and chatted for a while. Sam began telling me about the problems she'd faced during the evening. Sam started to let out a laugh, 'It's been a war zone, I had to put my tin hat on halfway through the night it was that bad'. We both burst out laughing. 'Well,' she said 'it's all over with now, we can put tonight down to experience'.

I looked around noticing the lounge was a lot bigger now that most of the people had gone. I could see more detail. My attention was drawn to the corner of the room where the DJ box stood.

Only one dim wall light illuminated this darkened area.

I sensed someone was watching me. Unseen eyes following every move I made. I could feel them burning into me. My instinct told me it was only a matter of time before I met their owner.

Our conversation on the charity night continued. I could see Sam had a genuine interest in what I did for a living. 'I would love to do your job, I think it's fascinating how you can see into other people's lives,' she said. I asked her if she had ever seen a ghost.

'Yes I have seen and heard things, in this pub, it's frightening working here when you are alone. You hear lots of things all the time, voices in the corridor at the top of the stairs and down in the basement. I looked into her dark brown eyes and could see the fear coming from within.

'It's happening nearly every day now, I am on edge most of the time and it's not just me who has seen things in here. Do you see the four men standing at the end of the bar?' I turned to look in the direction Sam was pointing. 'Can you see the bloke with a blue jacket on? That's Phil the owner and the tall lad standing next to him with a red t-shirt on? That's Christopher. He is a barman; he has seen loads of freaky things over the last couple of months. We can go and chat with them. Finish off your drink then I will introduce you.'

I thought that this could be the opportunity I needed to find out more and to see if Sam had been experiencing paranormal activity here. I needed to hear the full story from other people.

I picked up my stool and followed her to the end of the bar, she introduced me as one of the mediums that had been working that night. I noticed some odd looks pass between them but one by one, they shook my hand and gave me a warm enough welcome. Phil asked if I had enjoyed the night, 'Yes,' I said, 'It's been hard work, how much was raised?'

'It's gone great! We have raised over £1,500 for cancer research,' Phil said. He suggested I take part in a photo shoot for the local newspapers. I agreed it would be a good idea. We chatted for a few minutes, I glanced down at my watch 11:15 pm!

Oh God, I had to leave soon, Mark would be wondering where I am. He worried about me driving home alone in the dark. I picked up my mobile and rang the house, I waited for a few rings and was about to press the disconnect button when he finally answered.

'Hello?'

'Hi love...' I went on to explain to him about being so late, he wasn't happy about me why I was so late but I reassured him I wouldn't be long.

'I'll wait up for you,' he responded.

As I finished off the phone call, I felt relieved to know Mark and the kids were alright. With the news everything was alright at home I now didn't want to leave the pub. I felt that some kind of force was drawing me to the upstairs area. After what I had just experienced that night, I knew I couldn't walk away from this little girl. I carried on chatting to the owner of the pub and he introduced me to another barman Tony, who also worked as a DJ for the disco at the weekends. He was a funny character with a good sense of humour. I got on with him straight away, it was the same feeling I had with Chris. They seemed very down to earth. Tony started telling me about strange goings on in the pub and he said every one of the staff thought the Wheatsheaf was haunted. His experiences were very similar to Sam's. All the staff had heard noises, bangs and a little girl crying at the top of the landing.

Chris said, 'Did Sam tell you about what had happened in the kitchen a recently?'

I looked at him, 'No' I replied, 'She didn't mention anything about the kitchen.'

Chris then related the story about Sam's vodka jellies and the child's hand print.

'But how could a handprint be in the jelly,' I asked incredulously.

Sam knew she had locked the fridge door that night and the jellies were the first thing she took out the next morning after unlocking the fridge. Sam mentioned that the hairs on the back of her neck stood up on end every time she talked about it. Chris said 'We won't forget about that in a hurry!'

'Wow,' I said to Tony. 'Did you take a photo of the jelly?'

'We tried but you couldn't see it clearly. He said, 'You can ask anyone who works here, they all saw it with their own eyes.'

'That's amazing,' I said. We chatted more about the ghostly happenings that had taken place over the last few months. I didn't mention my own experience in the ladies' toilets because I wasn't sure it was right to share my story just yet but I was intrigued to hear other people's experiences. Feeling it was getting late I mentioned to Sam and Tony that I would be leaving soon.

'It's a shame you couldn't stop a bit longer... how about we take a look upstairs and I could show you the other rooms?' I looked at my watch thinking maybe I could squeeze in another fifteen minutes, so I accepted Tony's offer.

Tony stood up and made his way behind the bar reaching up to a grab a set of keys.

'Are we ready?' he said with a grin. Tony walked in front, fiddling with the keys, trying to find the one for the door in the corridor. As we walked up the stairs I could feel my heart pounding in my chest, I was expecting to see 'her' standing waiting for me at the top of the landing. Tony reached the top of the stairs and I was a few steps behind him. My instincts told me something was coming and I had better be prepared for it. A voice inside my head was repeating the words *'don't question what you will see... go with every emotion you feel'*. I shivered, felt faint and out of breath. Running my hands through my hair nervously, I asked my guides for help. *'Release this anxiety and be calm'*, they replied. At the top of the stairs I was standing in the exact place the little girl had appeared just a few hours ago. I saw Tony looking at me.

'Do you want to start from the toilets?' He asked, 'Then move on to the other rooms that are up here?'

'Lead on,' I said... my heart filled with anticipation. He pushed open the toilet door and I followed him down a couple of steps towards the room.

At the far right, there was a window directly facing me. I headed towards it and pulled back the netting to look out. I could see over the road, another pub named the Black Horse. It looked as old as the Wheatsheaf. To the left of the Black Horse, I could see that there were houses on both sides of the road. I could also see the entrance of the car park. Then it hit me! *The window I was looking from was the same one I'd first noticed on my arrival earlier that evening.* I let the netting fall back into place and followed Tony into the ladies' toilets. Walking back into the room I noticed it felt unnaturally cold.

Suddenly I was seeing the little girl's bedroom again. I was presented with flashes of light and detailed images. I could clearly see the wallpaper, the drapes at the window and the small bed. The only thing that was different was the little girl wasn't there. Not even her energy remained. After the room faded away I described all the details to Tony as he stood beside me listening in amazement. With Tony fully up to speed, I was now ready to explore further. We left the toilets and made our way to a door situated further down the corridor. 'Can we look in here now?' I asked.

I stood behind him as he put the key in the lock. I felt we were about to open Pandora's Box. Tony, turned and looked at me.

'Are you sure you want to do this?' he asked me cautiously.

'Yes,' I said firmly, 'I have to know what happened to the little girl.'

Tony pulled down the handle. The door opened inwards and we walked into the darkness.

'There's a light switch half way down the corridor,' he said, as we walked further along the pitch black corridor. I felt like a frightened child, the darkness closing in on me and wrapping itself tight around my body. Tony found the switch and turned on the light. My heart was racing, fuelled with adrenaline. I moved forward and stood beside Tony. He was next to a closed door.

'This is a bathroom,' I said. He looked surprised.

'How do you know there's a bathroom in there?' he asked. 'I believe I may have been here before in another time. I am certain this is a bathroom,' I said. Tony was clearly taken aback by the answer I gave him. 'Can I ask you a question? I could hear a tremor in his voice, 'Are you sure you've never been in this part of the pub before?' I stood beside him, looked him in the eyes and shook my head.

'This is the first time I have been in this area of the pub.' he replied, shaking his head. He unlocked the door and pushed it open. A bath and sink within confirmed the truth of my prediction. I turned to look at Tony and saw the look of disbelief etched onto his face.

'In the past, a few mediums have been up here. None had connected this strongly before. It's as if you know everything,' Because I'd been late arriving, I'd missed a tour of these rooms that Tony had laid on for the visiting mediums. I gave Tony a smile to lighten the atmosphere a little.

'Let's see what you pick up on along here' he said, pointing towards another closed door. As we got closer to the door, I just knew the room behind it was connected to the little girl. Suddenly a man came running menacingly down the corridor towards us. I froze, held my breath then regained some semblance of composure as I realized the man was from the spirit world.

'Tony,' I gasped trying to control my breathing. 'Don't move a muscle; we are not alone in this corridor.' I grabbed his arm holding on to him for reassurance, at the same time telling him what I was seeing. The colour drained from Tony's face... The man was dressed in miner's clothing, grey pants, a dull white shirt and a grey waistcoat. He had a rounded face and looked to be in his thirties. He now stood right in front of me. He didn't look frightening in close-up, I felt a warm energy and he had a kind face.

'I am Edward, don't be afraid, I want to help you.'

'Help me with what?' I asked. He told me that he had been looking after the little girl since he was murdered here and his body dumped into a well.

He kept saying, 'I'm not scared of Him.' I was pleading with my spirit guide to help me deal with the situation. A voice told me, *'go with your emotion.'* I told Tony who I was communicating with and he said that other people had also mentioned an Edward. Warning flashes of light returned only brighter this time. I felt I was trapped in a timeless void listening to Edward's voice.

He kept repeating, 'I'm not afraid of Him, He can't control me, I look after all the little souls here. ' He faded from view then the name Suzanne came into my mind, my name, Suzanne! At that moment, I knew that I could connect with the child, I felt the bond a mother might have with a daughter. The role Edward had set for me was the rescue of this poor little girl's soul.

I let go of Tony's arm and asked if we could move to the rooms ahead. Part of me didn't want to take another step forward but a separate part of me was intrigued to know more. We walked to the next door. Tony opened it and together we made our way in. I looked around; it was just a normal working kitchen with shelves and workbenches. For the first few moments I felt nothing, then a flash of light and sunshine burst in through a window. The walls were changing from being whitewashed to burgundy red wallpaper. I was now standing in a living room. A large desk was positioned in the far left of the room next to a window decorated with heavy cotton drapes. I gave Tony a running commentary of what I was seeing. I could smell the musty dry air hitting the back of my throat. I could see a black iron spiral staircase on the far side of the room. As I looked around, the image of the old living room changed and I found myself looking down the black spiral staircase at a long dark corridor which led to the lounge below. Before I knew it I was back in the kitchen again, in the middle of the room looking at Tony.

'Where has the big bay window gone' I asked, pointing towards the ovens and fans that were situated on the back wall. He was shaken and I didn't understand why. 'What's the matter Tony', I said. 'There used to be a window in here, but it's been boarded up for at least the last ten years,' he replied.

I heard a voice telling me that this was his room, he

was in charge of the pub. Two names then came to me, Kathleen and Elizabeth. I felt that Kathleen was connected to the little girl in some way, maybe her mother. There also was a connection with Dublin or thereabouts. I felt that Kathleen had died in childbirth, and the little girl had been sent over to Elizabeth in England, maybe around the early 1900's. Elizabeth was a relative, perhaps an auntie.

Again I was visited by flashes of yet more lights. I could see a group of men dragging another man out of the pub. They were shouting and swearing at him. I could hear their steel toe-capped boots scraping across the cobbled stones. Although it was dark I could see a man being forced away from the pub towards the main road. The men were shouting, telling him never to come back. I couldn't see his face, only his silhouette

I felt the bitterness and hatred he held inside. He had once been a man who had controlled everything and everyone. People feared his terrible temper.

Again, I gave Tony an account of everything as it happened. It was as I finished speaking, a strange coldness wrapped itself around my legs then crept up towards my shoulders. The feeling of someone's breath on the back of my neck became almost unbearable. I stood motionless, feeling an icy coldness sitting on my left shoulder, making me feel uncomfortable, and letting me know I wasn't welcome. I needed to get away. Tears were running down my face as I asked Tony if we could move out of the room.

'Okay,' he said, as he laid his hand on my shoulder 'Are you okay to carry on into the next room?' I bent forward slightly getting control my breathing.

'Yes I am fine now' I said, I wiping away the tears.

'Come on then,' he said, as we walked back out of the kitchen. looking up I could see an attic door set into the wall between the two rooms. I told Tony that I felt there was something very evil behind that door. He asked if I wanted to have a look, I firmly declined.

We headed towards the door on the right. I felt Edward's presence again. He seemed very anxious and started to pull me into the room.

'This is where we spend a lot of time talking and waiting for our prayers to be answered', he told me. Edward was agitated and apprehensive as if waiting for something bad to happen. The closer I got to the centre of the room, the greater I became tense and angry. Suddenly the lights came on. 'Sorry if I made you jump'... said Tony. I turned to see him standing a few feet behind me. The room was being used to store unwanted bits and pieces. I saw household furniture and lots of boxes. The colour scheme of the room was dreadful. A horrible dark green on the skirting boards, dirty magnolia wallpaper with a burgundy red frieze, and a black painted ceiling made the room feel extremely depressive. There was a large window framed with heavy red drapes which looked out towards the traffic lights.

I noticed Edward was now standing to my left, pointing to the chimney breast wall straight in front of me. A shiver ran up my spine as the scene before me changed. I was now standing in a kitchen area. I could see a big fireplace. The walls were a dark grey colour and a stout wooden table with six chairs stood in the centre of the room. The scene began to fade and return to normal. I hadn't picked up anything spiritual here

A moment later any warmth in the room vanished as a menacing darkness formed beside the chimney breast.

A tall heavy built man with ashen skin and short black receding hair manifested before me. His deep penetrating blue eyes were framed with dark circles making their colour seem more vivid. His face was a twisted mask of arrogance and contempt.

This vile man stared at me as if I were dirt on his shoe. I looked directly back at him. I was compelled to shout the name Joseph, and as the sound left my lips, a chilling scream reverberated around the room. I glanced at the floor tiles, they were changing into an old grey floor covering. The little girl appeared, peeping through golden curls to the open doorway, looking at the man that terrified her so. The sight of Joseph made the little girl run off in a blind panic. Down the corridor, she ran as fast as her thin little legs could carry her. She was desperately looking for a hiding place, trying to find an open door on the way. Dark clouds gathered in the skies above. Women pleading for their lives joined with noise of a growing storm outside. Men were shouting. Misery hung thickly in the air. The wretched child just kept running until she entered the room with the black spiral staircase. She took the stairs down two at a time but on reaching the floor below, a man was waiting for her. He took hold of her roughly, dragging her towards the cellar door.

I watched in horror as these terrible images played out before me. The child had met her fate the same way as many others had in this wicked place. Her little life extinguished, as easy as blowing out a candle.

I realized that Joseph was still staring intently at me. As I looked into those evil dead eyes, he was inviting me into the depths of his depraved mind. Dreadful scenes that nobody should ever witness appeared before me. The child lying like a ragdoll was lifted and placed into an old sack. I then saw the sack being pushed into a hole in the wall beside the fireplace where we stood. Joseph seemed to enjoy the horror I was feeling and gave me a slight smile before stepping backwards into the wall.

Distressed and shaking I shouted, 'The body of the

little girl is behind the wall,' I turned to find that Tony had been joined at some point by Sam, Phil and Chris. All their faces wore a look of astonishment. Sam was standing in front of me, tears streaming down her face. She touched my arm in a gesture of compassion. They all could see how upset I was and led me from the room trembling, the one thought that went with me was, Joseph thrived on darkness and other people's misery.

Downstairs in the bar, Sam and the others fussed around me offering kind words and a drink. When at last I settled down and my trembling subsided Phil, Chris, and Tony joined Sam and I at the bar. I could feel some uneasiness growing and I noticed some glances the four were making between each other. It was then Sam spoke. 'Suzanne we haven't exactly been up front with you.' 'In what way I asked?' 'Well...' she hesitated, 'We used the Quija board loads of times, probably for months before the vodka jelly thing' 'Ok' I said, 'but how does that concern me.' Sam looked to the others before continuing. 'We were getting stuff coming through that made no sense at the time. Names, details and things. During the same period, weird things were happening around the place. Bottles breaking on the bar. Glasses moving by themselves. Chairs and stools being shifted you know, just like in that Poltergeist Film'. 'I still don't see what this has to do with me' I said. Tony's answer to my question made the hairs on my arms stand on end. 'Well, one name kept being repeated almost every time we went to use the board. The name was Suzanne. Your name... Suzanne!'

I couldn't believe what I was hearing. I was aware my stomach had knotted into a tight ball.

'Yes' said Sam joining in. 'And when you turned up tonight and told me your first name I was shocked, all I had on my list of mediums was surnames and initials'. That's why I gave you such a funny look'. Tony chipped in, ' And all that stuff upstairs just now, you were saying things that I remembered coming through during our Ouija board sessions.'

The four of us discussed the happenings of the evening and Sam asked what we should do next. I told them I had to try and make contact with the little girl again and suggested that I could come back soon. All of them agreed this would be acceptable and we made arrangements for me to return on the 18th September. I said my farewells and left the pub. My head was spinning with thoughts of the little girl and her short sad life. Something else made it's way into my mind pushing other thoughts aside. A man called Joseph!

17th September
Dog Soldier

The whole experience at the Wheatsheaf caused changes in me that I was struggling to come to terms with. I carried an emptiness of loss within. Images of Joseph burst into my waking thoughts, making the day that lay ahead feel miserable and pointless. I had to force myself out of bed and try to shake off the darkness that had wrapped around me like a blanket. I dressed and began my normal routine but everything seemed slower. It was like walking through a thick fog. I was baffled by my depth of knowledge concerning the child from the previous day. *How did I know so much about her* I thought. Then there was Joseph. *What was that all about? Could one man be that evil? And why had he chosen me to see those awful images?* No matter how hard I tried, those thoughts kept returning to me throughout the rest of the day.

Even taking Francesca to school and back, looking after Alex or the mundane chatter from daytime tv couldn't distract me from my thoughts of the Wheatsheaf. During our evening meal, I just picked at my food. I gave Mark a brief outline of the charity night and he just listened in silence. Afterwards, I cleared the table while Mark settled himself on the couch to watch TV.

When I eventually got to sit down, Mark looked at me

and said, 'You look worn out love, I'll make a cuppa'.

He returned a few minutes later balancing a tray of two teas and a plate of biscuits.

'You look like you're carrying the troubles of the World on your shoulders love' he said.

'I'm fine, I just have a lot going on with that pub.' I tried to look reassuring, but from his expression, I could see that it hadn't worked.

'You know that whatever happens, I'll be here for you.' Mark said sympathetically.

His kind words released something inside. Tears were running down my face as I pulled Mark close. I sobbed like a baby with my head resting on his shoulder.

'Hey don't cry, you're better than that,' he whispered. 'God help the ghost in this pub, he won't know what hit him when you're finished with him.' I let out a little laugh. 'You'll eat him for breakfast!' He pulled away and wiped my eyes. 'I have a brilliant idea,' he said with a cheeky grin as he disappeared into the kitchen, returning with a DVD. 'This will totally freak you out,' he beamed. Always the film fanatic.

I looked at the cover 'Dog Soldiers?' I murmured.

'The ratings are mint! My mate Paul said he couldn't sleep in the dark for a week!'

'That's nothing new for Paul,' I remarked with a smile as we both giggled to ourselves. He put the DVD on and we snuggled into a blanket he'd grabbed from the chair, and prepared to be freaked out.

During the film I lost interest in the plot and my thoughts again turned to the little girl, that harrowing look on her thin face flashed before my eyes. Mark jumped suddenly which set my heart racing. He had been scared by something in the film. We both settled down again and we remained there together, on the couch, until the final credits of Dog Soldiers rolled up the screen.

I felt so tired. My body was aching and I could hardly keep my eyes open. When Mark suggested we have an early night I readily agreed. I made my way upstairs while Mark made sure all was secure for the night. When I peeked into Francesca's room, she was sound asleep, lying in a most awkward position, just like she usually did. Alex was tucked up in his cot, all snug just the way I had left him. Walking into the bathroom, I got myself ready for bed. The face looking back at me from the mirror appeared so tired. Giving a big sigh I turned off the light and went into the bedroom. I checked the window above my bed and made sure it was closed. Francesca liked to open it occasionally. Once I was sure everything was secure I got under the covers and laid my weary head on the pillow.

A slight noise made me raise my head. Mark was peering around the door, 'Don't you look snug,' he smiled and I beckoned him to bed. 'One minute, I need my pyjamas on.' I felt the mattress move as he climbed into bed. I opened my eyes and there beside me lay Spiderman! He was wearing the superhero sleep suit I had bought him some time ago. I couldn't help smiling as I turned off the bedside light. I was smiling! I hadn't done much of that over the last twenty-four hours. Exhaustion handed me into the welcoming arms of sleep and my weary body slowly unwound.

My dreamless slumber was broken by a faint tapping on the window behind me. 'What's that?' I murmured sleepily. I turned onto my back and listened closely. Nothing... the tapping had stopped.

I opened my eyes slightly and looked around the room. The temperature in the bedroom had dropped, turning my breath into a white mist that hung in the air about my head. The cold didn't feel natural. It was so intense. I tried to reach out towards Mark but found I couldn't move a muscle. Something was pinning me down. I tried to speak but all I could manage was a few gasps. I was screaming inside my head and all the while Mark slept peacefully beside me.

Then I heard it. The tiniest whisper, 'Help me, please help me'

It repeated over and over again getting louder each time. The little girl was begging for my help! The voice filled the bedroom. Using every ounce of strength I could muster I pushed up from the mattress and fell from the bed onto the floor. I saw her hanging there above the bed beside the window. Her head was bowed but I could see her small battered arms and legs, a corruption of black, yellow and blue bruises. I scrambled to my feet, 'I'll save you, I'm coming for you,' I shouted. I saw her thin little arms reach out to me as she began to fade from view. The Venetian blinds that covered the bedroom window were left swinging violently.

I was like a rabbit trapped in headlights. I stood there just staring towards the window until Mark's voice brought me out of my daze.

'I heard it! I bloody well heard it!' he shouted. I saw he was standing in the corner of the room with his back pressed against the wall. He ran to my side, put his arms around me and 'Let's get out of here, it's freezing!' I knew it wasn't just the cold that was making him tremble.

We went down the stairs and he placed me gently on the couch. Holding me close he said, 'It's okay Sue, I heard it too, everything! I can't believe it.' He kissed the top of my head and pulled me closer to him. 'You have to help her, she sounded so alone and frightened. I think we should spend the night down here,' he said. I didn't feel like going back up into that bedroom so nodded in agreement.

17TH SEPTEMBER DOG SOLDIER

Mark brought some pillows and blankets and then went into the kitchen to make a couple of cups of tea. The hot drink failed to remove the coldness inside of me. Mark pointed out it was 3 am. We had children to see to in the morning. I snuggled down into the couch and pulled a blanket over my head, trying to send the Wheatsheaf and all it's troubles out of my thoughts for a few restful hours.

18th September
Before the storm

My routine began as usual with the domestic side of life demanding my attention but all the while I couldn't stop thinking about the past few days. My mind replaying the experience of seeing the little girl on the top of the stairs; I knew I had to help her in some way. No matter what lay ahead, I knew I had been given the task of helping her. Joseph also came into my thoughts frequently. Each time seeming to leave some of his disgusting presence in my heart. There was a battle building between us. I just knew he wouldn't easily relinquish his hold on those poor souls at the Wheatsheaf. I needed to prepare for the encounter. Clearing away after breakfast I stopped for as moment, closing my eyes. A picture came into my head. I was seeing a beautiful green field with a statue of Our Lady standing at the centre. I was being guided to where I could find some help.

Leaving the kids with Mark after telling him I was popping out for a short while, I jumped into the car and headed for a village I knew well. Every time I pass the small town, it brings back so much of my past back to me. I started to smile to myself, *'Remind yourself of how far you have come.'*

I parked the car close to the old church I'd visited many

times over the years. The weathered heavy oak doors stood partly open offering a safe haven away from all the madness that surrounded me. Once my eyes had adjusted to the lower light level within, I took a moment, soaking in the peace and quietness. Only I stood in this comforting tranquillity. I walked down the aisle and sat in a pew at the front of the church. The face of Christ gazed at me from the Cross upon the altar.

Bowing my head in prayer I said in a whisper, *'Help me, God... Show me a way through these difficult times.'* As I sat there lost in thought, a feeling of warmth started to envelop me. A confidence was building inside. I was stronger. With relief, I knew I was up to the task before me. The visit to this old church had restored in me something that Joseph had almost removed. *'Faith!'*

On the return journey home, I felt like a new person. I would spend the rest of the day with Mark and the children. Anything concerning Joseph could go to hell for a few hours.

I picked up a few things at the local Co-op that I needed then headed for home.

Pulling up at the house I could see Fran at her bedroom window. On seeing my car she disappeared from the window and in the next moment was running down the front path to greet me, arms opened wide. I dropped the bag of shopping I was carrying and hugged her tightly.

Mark came to the front door carrying Alex in his arms.

'Do you fancy going out for a walk along the beach?' he asked.

Seeing the smile light up Francesca's face told me Mark's answer had to be yes...

'Come on then let's get our coats on, it will be fun!' I shouted.

Having a change of scenery was what I needed, and it

felt good doing normal 'family' things together.

At the beach, we had a great time. Even the biting wind from the North Sea couldn't spoil our pleasure. Mark and I watched as Fran ran along splashing in the water whilst our dog Holly leapt into the waves barking with excitement. Alex sat wailing in his pushchair wanting join them. It was times like this that made me appreciate the normality of family life.

At the beginning of May, I had decided to go full time with my mediumship and psychic work and was finding that the jobs of full-time medium and domestic goddess didn't mix too well.

After a couple hours, it was time to go home. We travelled in a happy silence, Fran and Alex sleeping on the back seat, Holly beside them and Mark watching out of the car window.

A glance at the time on the dashboard clock jolted me out of my pleasant bubble.

It wouldn't be long before I had to start getting ready for my evening ahead at the Wheatsheaf again!

The journey passed quickly and soon we were back in the house.

Mark seemed to pick up on my uneasiness. He took hold of my hands and asked, 'Will you be Okay tonight? 'I'll be fine' I replied with more confidence than I really felt. Releasing Mark's hands I pulled back. 'Alex needs a bottle, while I'm in the kitchen do you want a cuppa?' I said. 'Yes' came his reply, Mark had never refused a cup of tea in all the time we'd been together.

My phone rang just as I was pouring some juice for Fran. Mark walked into the kitchen carrying Alex on one arm and handed the phone to me. He told me it was Sam from the Wheatsheaf.

'Hi Suzanne, it's Sam.'

18TH SEPTEMBER BEFORE THE STORM

'Hi Sam, you ok?'

'Yes thanks, just checking that you're still coming tonight?'

'I'll be there by 9 o'clock, I'm still a bit shaken up though.'

'I bet you are, all of us here have been on edge as well.'

Sam went on to describe how jumpy everyone had been. 'We haven't even dare use the Ouija board since the charity night.'

'Good,' I replied. I had picked up on the fear in her voice.

God knows what the hours ahead held for us. A shiver ran down my spine at that thought. As we ended the conversation, I could a notice a little knot starting to grow in my stomach.

Time was ticking away. I was probably about to meet Joseph again and I had no idea how I was going to deal with him. Standing in the kitchen I closed my eyes and asked for guidance.

A plan began to form in my mind. Create a diversion for Joseph! One group enters the cellar and hopefully he turns up. Then you go upstairs to connect with the child. At least, it seemed like a good plan.

The evening meal passed in a blur. I sort of remembered cooking it but the eating bit of it had vanished from my memory. By the time I'd washed up and packed my bag for the evening ahead, I came back into the lounge. Mark, Francesca and Alex were sitting engrossed in a video

'What are you watching?' I asked Francesca.

She looked up at me and smiled. 'Monsters Inc. , it's my favourite.'

I shook my head and laughed. 'Every Disney film is your favourite Francesca.' I sat down beside her and we snuggled together. The video provided me with some light relief. As it ended I checked the time. 8:15 pm. Time to go. I quickly got ready, collected my bag and gave the kids a goodnight kiss because they would be in bed when I got back. Mark could see the apprehension written all over my face. 'Are you sure you want to do this?' he asked.

Part of me wanted to say 'No, I bloody well don't!' but deep down inside I knew what I had to do.

18th September
Team Building

The wind was getting stronger as I drove towards Boldon.

I found a parking space at the rear of the pub, switched off my engine and as I climbed out of the vehicle, I couldn't help but notice the moaning wind blowing through the trees that lined the back wall of the car park. It reminded me of the voices I'd heard on Wednesday night. Fear, sadness and utter despair.

Curiosity forced me to peer over the wall. I could just about make out the remains of an old well. I froze. A well! It all came back to me, Edward *told me about the well!! 'God that's where some of the bodies were dumped!'.*

The noise from the wind had increased as it blew through the trees. I turned to look at the building. Suddenly I was looking at it, as it had appeared way back in the early 1900's. I could see stables at the end of the building where now stood the top end of the car park. The lights were very dim.

A familiar scene started to play out before me. A group of men burst out of the pub laying kicks and punches onto a large man crouching in their midst. They told him never to come back to the village again. The man, just a dark outline to me, stumbled away from the group and the scene faded.

I recognised it as the same vision I'd had on the

Wednesday evening. I waited a minute or two to see if anything else occurred but everything looked like it was back to normal.

I made my way from the car park to the lounge door. Music from inside vibrated the glass in the window panes. Mmm... disco night at the Wheatsheaf... *just what I needed*. I decided to avoid the musical mayhem generated by the DJ and made my entrance via the top door which led straight into the bar.

Once inside I spotted the smiling face of Sam at the bar. She stood with Chris and Phil. Sam beckoned me over and above the racket from the lounge, she suggested we grab a table in the quiet corner of the bar to talk. The three of us sat at a table furthest from the lounge. I was eager to hear about any new relevant details. Chris began to recall an event that took place several months previously. 'It wasn't very busy and there were only a handful of customers in the pub. A loud banging sound made everyone looked towards a door at the end of the bar nearest the fireplace. A couple of the men who could see into the lounge from where they were sitting, shouted out, telling everyone a big fella had just stepped through a wall and was walking around in the lounge. He looked like a ghost! Some of the blokes stood up to see what was going on but quickly sat down when it looked like he was heading towards them. The man walked slowly into the bar staring at us. No-one moved an inch. We all just sat there getting paler by the minute. Then he was gone.'

'Oh my God! I said out loud'.

A flash of blinding light made me close my eyes. When I opened them everything looked so old fashioned and different from where I'd been sat only a minute or two earlier. The bar was a bit longer and further back. A number of men wearing caps and shabby clothes were

18TH SEPTEMBER TEAM BUILDING

standing having a drink. They looked like pitmen who had come straight from work, eager to quench their thirsts with a well-earned pint. Their blackened faces smiling as the amber nectar washed away the coal dust from their throats.

Suddenly my eyes opened to see Sam sitting beside me asking if everything was alright. 'Yes, I think so' I replied.

Phil was standing in front of me holding a glass of coke. 'Drink this, you will feel better soon'.

'Thanks,' I replied, my mind working in overdrive as I sipped from the glass. I didn't know how long I could endure the visions.

I noticed that John, the charity night organiser had arrived and was making his way over to our table. 'Hi John,' I greeted him. He didn't look in a particularly good mood. He sat down beside me and said, 'I'm worried about you Suzanne. From what I've heard, you're getting yourself in too deep here. Lots of things could go wrong and get beyond you.'

We both glanced at each other, 'Thanks for the concern John, but I have to do something here to help.'

'But how far are you willing go?'

'I don't know,' I said 'but I will give it my best shot.'

Chris joined into the conversation and started telling John some snippets of what had been happening at the Wheatsheaf. I noticed John's facial expression change when Chris shared with him the story of the man appearing in the bar.

Chris went on to say, 'After we'd used the board a few times and from things all of us had heard over the months, we'd got the impression a little girl was upstairs. I don't know why but I felt sorry for her... so one day I decided to get her a little doll in a basket.' As he told the story, goosebumps appeared on my arms. 'Well... I left the doll on the end of the pool table in the bar and locked up, only I had the keys that night. Next morning I opened up, turned the alarms off and walked back into the bar. It was so quiet I thought my hearing was playing up but I swear I thought I heard a child's laughter coming from the lounge. I ran through to the lounge but couldn't see anything. Just I was about to turn around and go back to the bar I saw it! There resting on the bottom step of the stairs leading to the toilets was the basket containing the doll! It still makes me shiver when I think of it.'

As we sat there, fascinated by the stories being told about the pub I noticed John's attitude towards me was quite demeaning and I felt a bit embarrassed in front of Sam and the others.

At closing time, Phil said we should move to the lounge because the disco had finished. Picking up our drinks we went through to the lounge and settled around a table near the back wall. I was surprised that about ten people had stayed behind after the pub closed to help us. Sam began the introductions. Including myself and Sam, there was Phil, his wife Laura, Denise, Chris, Maxine, John, and a couple called Rita and Dan. John and I put forward some ideas about what our goals were and how to achieve them. Everyone agreed that I should try and make contact with the little girl again but it was also recognised that Joseph could be a major fly in the ointment if he showed up whilst I did this. The group accepted my plan that John and I should begin by spiritually cleansing the pub as much as we could. Once that was complete one group would try and create a distraction in the cellar keeping Joseph busy whilst myself and the other group made an attempt to connect with the child upstairs.

18th September
Salt and Circles

I asked John if he was ready to begin the cleansing and he gave the thumbs up sign. 'Okay, let's go.' I said, picking up my bag. Sam handed me the keys to the main two rooms upstairs. As we made our way upstairs my breathing felt very laboured. My legs were like lead and the adrenaline pumping round my body seemed as though it would burst my eardrums.

After trying several keys on the bunch, John eventually found the one that opened the white door which led to the two rooms at the end of the upstairs corridor. The door creaked open and we looked into a black void.

'Are there any lights here Suzanne?' John asked. I told him where he could find the switches and soon the darkness was lifted.

Even though the light was on it still seemed dim and claustrophobic. Every nerve ending in my body was twitching. Any moment I imagined something terrible would appear. John looked at me as we walked together.

'You look awful Suzanne. I don't think you should do this,' he said,

'I'm fine' I replied not really believing my own words.

We arrived at two doors and John asked which room I wanted to enter. I pointed to the door on my left that was used as a storeroom. 'As you go in John, the switch is on the wall opposite the door. Be careful because there's a lot of stuff lying around on the floor.' He disappeared from view and I heard him curse as he stumbled over something in the room.

Out in the corridor I smiled at this but my smile vanished instantly as I realised there was an evil presence close by. I was aware of being watched, that unmistakable feeling of eyes following our every move.

When I stepped into the room the light was on and I could see how drab and tired everything looked. The worn drape hung over the bay window like a shroud. Boxes and old papers strewn about.

Discarded furniture was piled precariously high and there amongst all this junk ahead of me was the fireplace next to where I believed the body of the little girl lay!

John began moving things to make some space in the centre of the room. I joined in and an area of floor was quickly cleared.

Grabbing a carton from my bag I made a large salt circle on the floor.

My thoughts drifted to the image of that small body trapped behind the fireplace wall.

Suddenly I was seeing a repeat of the vision I'd had on Wednesday night. She ran into the room opened a drawer and removed the tin with the penny farthing design on the lid. She placed a small heart shaped locket with a silver chain inside the box. Screams outside the room became deafening. Other children clung close to me. Pure terror filled all their hearts. The misery was unbearable.

'STOP, I said to myself, 'I don't want to see anymore!!'

Tears flowed down my cheeks as the vision faded. John was stepping towards me, concern on his face.

18TH SEPTEMBER SALT AND CIRCLES

'I think you need to take a break Suzanne.'

I composed myself and replied, 'I'm fine, really'.

I dried my eyes and we continued preparing the room by placing a small crucifix at the doorway and splashing some holy water around the room. We lit some frankincense and myrrh oils in a burner then stepped into the salt circle. Holding hands we prayed for help and guidance. Quite rapidly the heavy oppressive atmosphere seemed to lift so we carried on repeating the process in the other rooms upstairs. We had visited most of the target areas upstairs when John said, 'Suzanne, you look like you could do with a break.' He sounded as if he cared, but each time he enquired into my wellbeing, I felt he was trying to highlight a weakness he thought he saw in me.

'I could do with a drink.' I agreed. 'You go on down, I just need to slip to the ladies then I'll join you.'

As I entered the toilets my stomach was doing somersaults. I went to the wash hand basins and took a cassette recorder from my bag. I set it up and started it recording. Maybe the tape would capture something interesting. Stepping backwards I took a moment to ask my guides for a connection to the girl.

'When the time is right', came back the reply.

Everyone was sitting around a table as I entered the lounge from the stairs. As I sat down with the group, Laura spoke up and said, 'You have the support from all of us here tonight and we take this seriously, we believe in you, Suzanne.' I thanked Laura for her encouraging words.

I noticed a light had appeared beside the lounge bar but no-one else seemed to have seen it. I could make out the shadowy outline of a man standing there close to where the entrance to the cellar was. I could feel malice coming from where he stood as he listened to us talking. Although he gave me the impression that he wasn't a good guy I knew that he wasn't Joseph. I could cope with the unwelcoming presence this man was radiating, despite the thoughts of *'Get Out, Get Out'* were being projected into my mind. I was much more fearful of what might appear in the opposite corner to where we sat, the corner where the DJ had his presentation stand. This area I had named 'Joseph's corner' because this was where I could feel his presence the strongest. I hoped he would stay away a little longer until everything was ready for me to make contact with the girl.

John snapped me back to the present by asking what I wanted to do next. I began by saying, 'We need to make a safe circle in here. Somewhere we can all feel safe and protected from this Joseph or anything else that wants to try and harm us'. John agreed and I began the task of making a spiritual safe zone for protection.

John and I sprinkled salt in a circle around our seating area and together we offered up a prayer of protection. I then invited everyone to join me inside the circle bringing with them thoughts of love and peace. I prayed for help from the angels, asking that they shine their pure light to cast out darkness and shelter those within the circle from harm.

The cleansing in the lounge continued. I carried burning incense and a small bible. John wafted smoke from a Native American smudge bowl. We gave every nook and cranny our attention. The coldest spot seemed to be around Joseph's corner. John looked at me as we both experienced a tension building up around us.

I asked Sam if we could get the heating put on and Phil went away to carry out my request.

After about fifteen minutes, the temperature was making the lounge more comfortable and everyone seemed relaxed. I had quickly taken to Sam's friend Denise. I could tell she too was psychic. *'It's good to be around genuine people,'* I thought.

'Are you sure she is in the wall upstairs?' Maxine asked. There were many feelings bouncing around inside of me and when I spoke, the words came bursting out. 'Am I sure? ... I have seen the girl stand before me, begging for help, I have watched her sobbing and running in terror. I watched as she was captured and carried away to suffer God knows what, and each time, I lived that fear with her. I saw her lifeless body wrapped in a sack, being pushed into the wall upstairs. All these images were as real to me as you are now. Yes I'm sure!' Maxine just stared at me her question had been answered. My nerves were jangling.

I asked if anyone would like to get the audio tape from the Ladies toilet upstairs and Chris volunteered. While he was away Sam revealed how the use of the Wheatsheaf Ouija board started. Apparently a ball of flame shot out of the fireplace in the bar one day stunning the customers there. 'It was the most frightening thing I'd ever witnessed in the bar. It was packed with people and everyone just stopped still for a minute. The ball of flame hovered for a few moments then shot back up the chimney. Everyone started talking again and the bar returned to normal. It was after the ball of fire we wanted to know what was going on, so someone suggested using the Ouija board. I'm not kidding when I say all of the staff were curious to know who or what was haunting the place.'

I was still trying to absorb the story of the ball of fire when Chris returned and laid the cassette on the table. Sam was the first to pick it up as she eagerly rewound the tape and pressed play. There was just a hissing sound and nothing else so she rewound it, pressed play, and held it to her ear. I watched her face for clues to what she was hearing. Suddenly she said 'My God!, stopped the tape and took it back a little then pressed play again. My heart began to race as I asked. 'What is it Sam?'

'Wait a second' she replied, stopped the tape, then rewound and played the section again. The colour had drained from her pretty face. 'You need to hear this Suzanne, here listen'. Everyone seated around the table leaned forward as I took the cassette from her and held it to my own ear. A couple of seconds after pressing play and listening to a hissing sound, I could just make out a deep manly voice speaking words that made my blood run cold.

'I am coming for you Suzanne' the voice growled menacingly.'

18th September
Reaching Out

It took me some moments to gather my thoughts after hearing the threat on the tape. Instinctively I knew that was Joseph's voice. *'Well'*, I thought, *'I'm not going down without a fight mate.'*

I announced what the content of the tape had been and I think that was the point when everything dropped to a new level of fear within the people who sat with me.

With Joseph's threat still whirling around my thoughts, I felt the need have one last walk around downstairs before beginning the vigil upstairs. I told every one of my intentions and made my way through the lounge and into the corridor that linked the lounge to the bar. My eyes had difficulty adjusting to the darkness. I walked slowly for fear of tripping. Despite the lack of light, I knew I was headed towards the area where the managers' office was. A blinding flash of light hit my eyes and I fell to the ground. I lay in the corridor pinned down by some unseen force. The darkness lifted slightly and once more I was watching as the terrified thin little child ran down the spiral staircase that led near to where I lay.

I felt so helpless just watching as a figure stepped from the shadows at the bottom of the stairs and grabbed her pale weak arm. The man took her by the throat with his other hand and was squeezing it tightly. Her small legs buckled beneath her and the man swept her up into one of his arms. She made one final struggle and opened her mouth to scream, and a piece of sacking was pushed roughly into her open mouth. Her muffled choking grew fainter as he disappeared towards the cellar door. Then they were gone. I looked around but all I could see was the darkness of the corridor. I was filled with anguish for the girl, my whole body shaking with fear and hatred for the man. *'You must make the connection with her now'* I said to myself. I managed to stand and still shaking made my way back into the lounge.

John looked me up and down as I joined the group. 'You look a bit shook up Suzanne, seen a ghost?' he said laughing at his own joke. Nobody present appreciated his poor attempt at humour. The group was more concerned I was alright. 'It's time' was all I could say.

We split into two groups. Sam and Denise had a bit of an altercation about who was going to which group, but quickly reached a mutual agreement.

Phil, Sam, Rita and Dan were in John's party and Denise, Chris, Laura and Maxine made up my group. Phil had given John and I the Pub's two walkie-talkies so we could keep in touch with each other.

I checked my bag to make sure I had everything I needed then my group headed towards the stairs leading up to the first floor.

I saw John and his group moving across the lounge to where the cellar entrance was.

I may have appeared calm outwardly, but inside my heart felt like it was going to burst out of my chest. We huddled close together as we climbed the stairs. Every shadow suggested something evil. The temperature was starting to fall again. Soon I could see my breath in the air.

18TH SEPTEMBER REACHING OUT

A damp coldness touched our faces. At the top of the stairs, we turned into the corridor that led to the storeroom. One of the group suddenly sneezed and we all jumped then laughed nervously. I took the group into the room John and I had prepared earlier. I pointed to the salt on the floor and asked them to sit within the circle. As we sat there cold and scared, Chris said, 'I thought it might be a good idea to bring this,' and held up the doll he'd bought for the child months ago. We placed the doll at the centre of the circle. Denise and Laura said they would take turns making a video recording with Laura's camera. Maxine sat ready to take notes of anything that happened. I settled down into a state of relaxation that was only possible with the help of my guide. I was sinking into myself. My awareness was changing. Those around me faded away and I entered an altered reality. I was in a place where space and time had no meaning. She was close.... . I heard my own voice speak. 'I am your friend'. Silence. 'We are here to help you'.

Silence. 'We will not hurt you'. Everyone near was holding their breath. A floorboard creaked. 'Come to me little one' I said softly.

Silence. 'You will be safe here'. I thought I heard a faint shuffling sound in the corridor outside. Hairs rose at the back of my neck. 'We want you to meet the angels'. A light sigh. I looked towards the door. She was there!

Her small frame, standing still at the doorway, but with her back towards me. 'Join me in this circle of love. We have made especially for you' I begged. Maxine was scribbling furiously. Denise and Laura for some reason had stopped the video recording and just sat watching with open mouths. 'We have brought you a nice dolly, see, it's here in our circle. It's yours. Please take it'.

She slowly turned...

'Come and get the dolly'

'Leave it, Leave it'. A chorus of long dead voices seemed to whisper from the shadows.

'The dolly is here. Just come into the circle and pick her up'.

The whispering countered, 'Do not listen, Stay with us'.

She raised her head. I saw her face properly for the first time.

Cruel laughter echoed from somewhere in the dark corners of the room, enjoying my horror as I gazed at her poor tortured little face.

Wound round that beautiful small head, crushing her golden locks, was a blindfold. It looked painfully tight and soaked with what appeared to be many hours of tearful agony. All my emotions welled up and choked in my throat.

She walked, frail arms outstretched towards the doll, shuffling her bruised beaten little legs, the blindfold not hampering the slow but sure progress to where we sat. Timidly she stepped forward into the circle reaching for the doll. She had the beginnings of a smile on her sad little face. The temperature was ice cold.

Suddenly there was a loud crackle as the walkie talkie burst into life.

Denise was speaking 'John says Sam's hysterical and his group are getting out of the cellar as fast as they can. They'll meet us back in the lounge.'

The little girl was gone. There was little point in staying upstairs besides we were all desperate to find out why Sam had freaked out.

When we arrived back in the lounge I saw Sam. She was curled up in a ball on a seat in the safe area. I immediately went to her side. She was trembling. 'He placed his hand on my face. It was horrible' she sobbed.

18TH SEPTEMBER REACHING OUT

'You mean Joseph?' I asked. Sam described the most disgusting feeling she had ever experienced. 'It was a man's hand. The way it touched my cheek made me feel as if I was being violated. It felt like he was touching me all over my body. It was evil and made me feel dirty. I couldn't stay there a second longer. Sorry.'

'It had to be him' I thought. For the next ten minutes I sat with Sam getting her back to some sort of normal state. Then it was John's turn to answer my questions. 'How the hell did that happen to Sam' I demanded. 'Why didn't your protective circle work?'

'I dunno' he mumbled. 'Maybe whatever was down there was too strong to keep out of the circle' he said.

Phil must have overheard the conversation and came over. 'What circle John? We never did that. You stood outside the cellar doors for ages whilst saying prayers and stuff before we even went in. We'd only been in there about five minutes when you were saying that you thought it was a load of rubbish and we should go back. That's when Sam screamed and fell to the floor.

Me and Dan had to help her out because you shot past us through the door like a rocket.'

Fearless John the Medicine Man, had shown his true colours. 'A whiter shade of yellow' it would seem.

For some time we all just sat quietly in the safe area. The wall clock showed 5.30 am. It was almost dawn. Without warning, Sam stood up and stepped out of the circle. I thought she needed the loo. When she returned a few minutes later in her right hand was a brick hammer. She was walking quickly towards the stairs. 'Where are you going?' shouted Phil. Sam didn't answer but her pace up the stairs quickened. Phil shouted again. 'Sam, Sam can you hear me?'

She just kept climbing the stairs. Phil, John and myself

ran after her but she was out of sight by the time we got to the top of the landing.

A noise coming from the storeroom at the end of the corridor told us where she was. In the short time she'd been in there Sam had managed to knock a small hole in the wall to the left of the old fireplace. When the three of us reached her, the hammer lay on the floor next to her feet. She was tearing at the bricks with her bare hands. 'I must find her' she was sobbing. 'Leave it Sam' said John, 'You'll find nowt in there but bricks and dust'. I glared at him. Any respect I'd had for this man had gone. 'Couldn't he see how distressed she was.' The event in the cellar had obviously had a more profound effect on Sam than any of us had realised. We gently walked her back downstairs. It felt like things were over for the time being. As the group began to disperse I sat there in the lounge mulling over what had happened that evening.

I believed the girl was still trapped here, but why? An image came into my mind of the child placing a locket in the tin box she kept. It was the locket! She had run away down the stairs but left the locket behind. It must hold some special significance to her. She couldn't leave without it.

My thoughts were interrupted. Phil made some welcome cups of tea and placed them on the table where Sam and I sat. The three of us sat, each lost in our own thoughts. Just as the clock showed 6. 32 am we made arrangements for the group to meet again on Monday evening. Phil said he would get in touch with the others and let them know.

I carried my weary body out to the car park and climbed into my car. I sat for a moment looking at the Wheatsheaf.

'You will never keep her Joseph' I thought, then turned the ignition and drove off.

20th September
Sadness Grows

It was 5.0 am and I laid wide awake. Each time I closed my eyes his face came into sight. Another night of Joseph forcing his way into my thoughts. I could make out the sheen of sweat on his brow as he eagerly made his way to the cellar, excitement building inside as he anticipated the perverse pleasures he would share that evening.

The thought of returning to the Wheatsheaf filled me with dread. It was facing with the unknown that was so difficult to handle. The only thing I knew deep inside was, a confrontation lay ahead and my nemesis was Joseph.

I laid there thinking things over. What had compelled Sam to break down that wall? She acted as though possessed. Tearing at the brickwork with her bare hands. Then there was the audio tape and Joseph's threat to me. He wanted me. Did I have the strength to stand up to the depraved beast? It all seemed too much for me to cope with. I didn't know when the tears had started but I laid sobbing. My crying woke Mark. He sat up, put his arms round my shoulders, and I quietly wept against his chest. 'You should talk to me Suzanne. You're bottling everything up. Tell me how I can help'. He was pleading with me. I could never share the torment with anyone. It was mine alone to endure. He stroked my hair, dried my eyes then held me tightly. We stayed like that for several minutes. My head was throbbing. I went to get out bed. Mark asked what I was doing. 'I need something for this headache' I replied. He told me to stay where I was and headed down to the kitchen, returning with a couple of paracetamol and a glass of water. After a several attempts, I managed to dispose of the tablets and hoped I would feel some benefit quickly.

Mark sat down beside me on the bed, gathered his pillows and placed them behind me. 'Right,' he said, 'From the beginning, tell me what's made you so upset.'

I told him of John's obnoxious attitude and how he'd been more of a hindrance than a help. I described my visions of Joseph and how fearful I had become. I spoke of the warning on the tape and the pathetic sight of the blindfolded child. I gave Mark as much detail as I could remember.

I could see Mark was taken aback.

'He had her blindfolded Mark.' It broke my heart to revisit the visions of her suffering, the short futile life she had lived, and the inevitability of her death.

'Please don't let these horrible things change you Suzanne. Promise me that if you are not strong enough to carry on, you will leave it alone and walk away'. I wanted to reassure him but knew this was a promise I couldn't make. I avoided a direct answer by kissing him on the cheek and saying 'I'll be alright love, honest'.

Mark seemed satisfied with my reply, looked at the clock and informed me it was 7 am.

'Right then! Let's go wake up our little tribe and headed out of our bedroom.

In the kitchen I kept my mind occupied, pulling Francesca's uniform from the dryer and heating milk up for Alex. I could hear him squealing upstairs. He was never good in the mornings and his morning crying sessions were the 'norm' in our house.

Mark came through the kitchen doorway carrying Alex in his arms. I looked at them both. *Two peas in a pod them two*, I thought. 'You can never say he's not yours' I laughed.

Mark looked at me and smiled, 'I'll make sure Alex is cleaned up, if you get Fran up and ready for school.'

Fran was all stretched out and sound asleep, she was never easily woken. She looked so peaceful it felt almost mean to wake her up. 'Come on Fran', I called to her. On the third attempt, her little face popped up from under the bedcover. I leaned down and kissed her forehead she wriggled and slightly opened her eyes, 'Hi Babe,' I whispered. She rubbed her eyes, still half asleep and looked up at me.

'Can I have a cuddle Mummy?'

'Of course, move over then.' She peeled back the quilt and rolled towards the wall leaving a little space for me. The bed was soft and cosy, but the fluorescent shade of pink on her Hello Kitty bed sheets was much too bright for the morning. I pulled her into my arms and stroked her hair, one hand on her chest, I could feel a calm heartbeat, the rhythm made me feel that all was right with the world. Just the two of us together and the warmth between us made me wish I could stay like this all day and sleep away my troubles. Special moments we shared were becoming less frequent as she was always out playing with friends in the park across the road.

'Come on babe, it's time for you to get ready for school,' I said softly, pushing my worries and exhaustion to the back of my mind. She rolled over and looked at me with her puppy dog eyes. She knew I wouldn't say no to an extra five minutes in bed. I spent the time catching up with all the stories about her friends and the daily routine of school. At that moment, life seemed more fun. I was so glad she had settled in well. It had only been a couple of months since we had moved to our new address and she already had made many friends. Her school grades had also improved. I glanced at her bedside table a book caught my eye. I picked it up.

'Oh, Mummy! That's "Goose Bumps!" I get them out of the school library... They are amazing!'

I looked at the picture on the front cover and quickly concluded it was a horror book.

'Are you sure you should be reading this?' I quizzed.

'Of course' she beamed. 'They are really popular and cool!'

'They won't be cool when you are having nightmares! Come, it's time for school.' I gathered her school uniform together placing it on the dresser. 'It's going to be cold today, so you need to dress warmly,' I said.

'Okay Mummy, I'll get dressed now,' she replied.

I left the room, thinking about how independent Fran really was, I didn't want her to be, but it was happening all so fast.

I made my way back downstairs to see Alex in the high chair with a mouthful of porridge, giggling at the telly as usual. He saw me come into the room. He waved his little hands about, almost knocking the bowl from Mark's grasp. Mark suggested a nice walk up to the school as a family. I could tell he didn't want me to be left at home alone. I agreed, knowing the break would be good for me. I had arranged several appointments connected to my business during the day but I didn't have the heart for them. A couple of quick phone calls made them disappear and my day became something bearable.

'I'm glad you did that' said Mark. 'You need a morning

off,' he smiled. After seeing Fran into school the walk back home from was so peaceful and refreshing. It felt good to take a relaxed stroll with Mark and Alex.

The rest of the day flew by so quickly. I'd managed to snatch some sleep, sorted through paperwork and watched Alex sitting on the floor playing with his toy cars. I saw he was ready for his afternoon nap so I picked him up and cradled him in my arms.

Suddenly the phone rang. I quickly answered it, trying not to disturb Alex now sound asleep in my arms.

'Hello,' I whispered.

'Hello Suzanne, it's Sam.' As always, she sounded enthusiastic. 'How are you doing?' she enquired.

I told her I was fine and we got into a conversation about the events that had occurred on Saturday night.

'If I'd received a threat from Joseph like you got, you wouldn't have seen my heels for dust!' she laughed.

'Oh, by the way, I managed to put the photos from the other night onto a disc, so bring your laptop over, we can have a good look and see if there is anything interesting. I finish work at 5 pm, so I am free to have a good natter.'

Eager to see what might be on the photos, a feeling of excitement came over me. We agreed to meet up at 5 pm and as we ended the call I could tell Mark wasn't happy. He'd listened to my conversation with Sam.

'I thought you weren't going over until about 9 pm?' he snapped.

'I told Sam I'd get there for about 5 pm, she has lots of photos from the other night she wants to show me.'

'So ... it looks like I'm making the tea for the kids again!' He said sharply as he stormed off into the kitchen.

'Mark, you know full well that I have to do this! Please don't be like this,' I pleaded with him. 'You even agreed it was right that I should help her!'

'You are becoming obsessed with the Wheatsheaf. Just remember you have a family here that needs you!' he shouted from the kitchen then slammed the door with a loud bang. Alex woke up with a start and immediately started crying. I lifted him up and tried to settle him into sleep again. I felt hurt that Mark had bottled up so much resentment towards me.

'Is he alright?' Mark's voice came from the kitchen.

'Yeah, but no thanks to you' I snapped back at him!'

As I calmed down, I began to understand Mark's anger. The Wheatsheaf and its ghostly inhabitants were becoming a massive strain on our relationship, and our family life was suffering. We had both become victims of the Wheatsheaf.

There was nothing left to say to him on the matter. It was probably better to let things settle and leave the subject of the Wheatsheaf alone for a while.

The sky began to darken as I drove to the school to pick up Francesca. By the time I was walking through the school gates the rain was pouring down. That just added to my bad mood.

I heard the school bell ring signalling an end to the academic day and very soon children were emerging from the main doors of the building.

My beautiful girl was running towards me, 'I made this for you Mum,' she said excitedly handing me a colourful trinket box that was overflowing with glitter. I was delighted that she made me this gift and surprised at how it lifted my spirits. I bent down and gave her a big hug. We ran back to the car with coats over our heads, climbed in, and closed the doors on the rain. I turned on the engine and turned the heater to full power. It felt good. The warm air was blowing on my face and through my hair.

'Are you going out tonight mum?' she asked, cause I

really want to watch the new Barbie film with you.' I reached over and grabbed her little hand.

'I'm sorry love, I've a few things to do tonight.' Her face dropped. I could see how sad she was.

'I'll make it up to you. How about you and I go out at the weekend and get those shoes you wanted?' Her face lit up.

'Yeah!' she replied with a satisfied smile.

'Come on then, let's get some shopping in.'

We were probably only in ASDA for about forty-five minutes but I still managed to spend over one hundred pounds. The contents of my purse did not look healthy.

The rain hadn't let up and the drive home felt miserable.

By the time we were unloading the car I only had about an hour left before setting off for West Boldon. Mark came out to help with the carrier bags and I could still sense the tension in him.

I told him I had to leave shortly and he said he would make tea for the kids. I could tell from the tone in his voice he wasn't happy.

I went upstairs and started to get ready. A very sad feeling grew inside of me when I thought about how our relationship had changed over the past few days. Mark and I were drifting apart and the arguments were becoming more frequent. It was only a matter of time before the whole damned Wheatsheaf thing destroyed us forever.

20th September
Intimidation

I parked up in my usual spot near the side entrance, I could feel a dark energy pushing down on me with every step I took. I gathered my bags and set them down and once again I stood there in the car park, memories flooding back to me. I glanced up at the window of the ladies' toilets, it felt like only five minutes ago since I had left this place and it was exhausting to know I had been there nearly every night over the past week. It felt like an eternity.

With weariness heavy in my heart, I walked towards the building. The evening was drawing in and it was slowly getting darker. I had taken these happenings to a personal level, but why? Other paranormal events I'd dealt with in the past had never affected me like this one. I knew there must be more to it. The story had no connection to me whatsoever. I had unanswered questions rolling around in my head, the ouija board... my name being mentioned, the strange link I seemed to have with the little girl.

Making my way into the lounge I saw the place was empty. Glancing up the stairs a lump formed in my throat as I recalled my first encounter with the girl, on the landing above.

'Hi!' Sam called out when she spotted me approaching. 'I am so pleased to see you, how are you doing?' She lifted

20TH SEPTEMBER INTIMIDATION

the bar hatch and dashed towards me. I was pulled into a warm hug.

'Sorry I'm late Sam, I got held up with things,' I said.

'It's okay, don't worry.' She pulled back with a smile and returned behind the lounge bar.

I placed my laptop on the counter and took a sip from the drink Sam had provided.

'I didn't know if you would come back? I just can't believe those threats from Joseph, they have made me so worried about you. It's given me nightmares.' I squeezed her hand and asked how everyone had been doing. Once up to speed on everyone, the topic shifted to the hole in the wall that Sam had made.

'Well... Chris has been hacking at it since Sunday night, and he's coming back tonight. We are all behind you Suzanne.' She held my hand tight. 'We just want to put this poor little girl to rest.'

I was so relieved and felt reassured to know that they were behind me, despite John's efforts trying to embarrass me. He had made me doubt myself. None of us had a clue about what we were facing or where it was going to lead.

As I stood at the lounge bar waiting for Sam to finish work my excitement was growing. I was hoping there would be lots to see in the photos Laura had given to Sam.

'I'll go get the disk from my car,' said Sam. 'You can have it all ready for me to look at when I finish.' 'I'll be two minutes,' she said chirpily as she left.

The place grew still and eerily quiet. I was standing looking through to the bar. Two men were sat talking and enjoying their pints oblivious to me watching them. All of a sudden, a man walked up and stood right behind me, my instinct told me not to acknowledge him, but I could feel him standing there hovering over me. I turned to see a stocky built man wearing jeans, a blue shirt and a black leather jacket. I noticed he had bad eczema on his face. He leaned towards me and I could feel his arm pressing firmly against mine.

'What do you want?' I asked.

Ignoring my question, 'Is there any staff in here?' he bellowed.

'She won't be a minute,' I replied while trying to avoid eye contact.

He mumbled to himself and then glared at me. I sensed his anger boiling up inside him and thought it was aimed mainly towards me. The atmosphere between us grew very cold as he continued to stare at me. I felt a familiar shiver run down my back, as I realized I hadn't heard him coming in; the doors usually slam when you pass through them. The only way he could have come in was through the passage behind the bar.

Standing very close to me in the lounge, he glared with hatred filling his eyes. Pressing himself against the side of my body his leather jacket felt cold on my arm. I pulled away.

'What are you playing at?' 'Stop leaning against me!'

'Have you got a problem with that?' he spat aggressively. I felt very uncomfortable with him even though I had put some space between us. He just stood there smirking.

'If you know what's good for you, get lost' I whispered under my breath as I tried to figure out where he had come from.

'What did you say? Get lost? Who do you think you are? You think you know everything? What do you think you know?' He waited a moment and when I didn't answer he bellowed, 'I'm asking you... what... do... you... know? I'm curious… what do you know?'

'Why are you being like this? Who are you anyway?' I asked.

'I'm your worst bloody nightmare!' he moved closer again. I heard the lounge door slam and was more than pleased to see Sam coming back in towards the bar. My obnoxious antagonist was leaning against me, shoulder to shoulder. I tried to slide away.

'Stop leaning on me' I demanded.

'Why? Am I making you nervous?' he sneered, enjoying the sight of me feeling uncomfortable.

'I've got it Suzanne!' said Sam waving the CD with excitement.

Then she noticed the man standing next to me. First she looked at him then me and an expression of confusion spread across her face. She clearly didn't know who he was.

'This man wants serving. ' I said pointing at him.

'Hello, what can I get you?' she smiled brightly.

'About bloody time, I'll have a bottle of Rose, the best one you've got... and two glasses,' he demanded. 'Less of the chat and just serve will you, my date will be here soon.'

'There is no need to talk to her like that,' I remarked sternly. 'She's only trying to be friendly!' I could see my remark hadn't pleased him much.

Sam opened the bottle of wine and put it on the bar in front of him with two glasses then waited for payment.

He handed her a ten-pound note and she gave him the change trying not to make contact with his hands. To my relief, he picked up the wine and made his way to Joseph's corner, but I suspected there would be more to come from him before the night was out. My heart was beating rapidly.

I looked at Sam and asked, 'Who is he? I wouldn't like to meet him in a dark alley.'

She just shook her head and said, 'I have never seen

him before, I don't know who he is.' I could feel his eyes following every move I made.

'Suzanne he's staring at you.' Said Sam.

I jumped when he slammed the wine bottle down on the table. Sitting in that corner he reminded me of Joseph, the resemblance was uncanny. I was shaking, I had really felt intimidated by that man.

'Where the hell did he come from?' she asked.

'I don't know Sam, he just appeared, breathing down my neck.' I could still feel his greasy presence clinging to my clothes.

'God help his date,' I smiled taking a sip of coke.

'What did you just say?' he shouted over. His voice echoed across the empty room.

'It was nothing about you mate' I said, as I turned to look at him.

'It better not have been!' he said, then took a drink. I ran my fingers through my hair and decided to head for the ladies' room. 'Hang on to my drink, I'll be right back,' I said to Sam, I could see him out of the corner of my eye. He was hunched over the table, sipping his wine, glaring at me as I crossed the lounge.

As I reached the top of the stairs, I could still feel his eyes on my back as I walked out of sight. Standing inside the ladies' toilets, I took a few deep breaths to steady myself. I had the impression he hated not just me, but all women. He was completely overbearing,

Heading downstairs I looked over the banister. *Oh my God, he's coming up the stairs. We had to pass each other on the stairs.* I was fearful that if we were alone he might hurt me. I sweating profusely and terrified of this horrible man. He climbed the stairs towards me so I stepped back to let him pass. He just stood there in front of me staring right into my face He tried to push me backwards. I could feel his breath on my neck as he towered over me. The only thing I could think of was to try and push past him so I half turned, elbowed him hard in the ribs and sprinted downstairs into the lounge. I ran over to the bar where Sam was standing. My heart was in my mouth.

'Are you alright Suzanne?' She came around the bar and stood beside me.

'No Sam, I'm really not, this isn't good.'

'As soon as he heard you coming down the stairs he shot out of his seat before I could move.'

'Who the hell is he Sam?'

'I've no idea Suzanne, but he gives me the creeps.' Right, just go sit at a table with your laptop, I've finished work now, so I'll sit beside you to make sure you're not alone with him.'

I moved towards the table and unzipped my laptop bag but I felt like picking up my belongings and driving home.

'I feel like I need a ciggy,' I said.

'No Suzanne, don't go outside... he might follow you again!. All of a sudden I heard a loud bang. I jumped and looked over to the source of the noise. He had entered the lounge again and moved closer to me. The noise had been his bottle being slammed onto the table next to me. 'Why are you sitting there now?' I asked.

'I can sit anywhere I damn well please,' he smirked sipping his wine. I lowered my head and diverted my attention to the laptop. I could still see him out of the corner of my eye, just staring at me.

'Is he bothering you?' Sam asked deliberately raising her voice. 'Chris is on his way; he will be here in five minutes.' It was good to know that another friend was on the way.

'My date will be here any minute,' he remarked.

'I'm not interested,' I murmured.

'I don't care what you think,' he glared at us, over his wine glass. He had already drunk half the bottle. I just wished he would leave so we could continue looking at the photographs. We half-heartedly flicked through a few but I wasn't able to concentrate. My attention was on the strange man gulping his wine.

Looking at the photographs I noticed orbs present in some of the rooms. Little faces seemed to be in each one. One picture in particular, caught my eye. It had been taken when I was doing the spiritual writing with Maxine. In the photograph she was leaning over and reading out questions to me whilst I was holding a pen and writing. I looked closer and I could just make out an image of the blindfolded little girl. She seemed to be holding the pen I was writing.

'Sam look!' I remarked, pointing at the child's ghostly figure in the photo.

'Oh my God, it's her!' said Sam.

We were so engrossed in the photographs, Sam and I were suddenly aware of a shadow being cast across our table. The awful man had risen from his seat and was standing right next to our table.

'What is it now?' I snapped.

'You think you're so clever don't you... little girl?' He spat in such a venomous tone.

'Yeah, I do think I'm clever so stop bothering me and my friend' I retorted firmly. Adrenaline was rushing through my veins as he leaned towards me. I could smell his hot sickly sweet breath fill my nostrils.

'You have a big shock coming your way little girl,' he whispered in my ear and then walked from the lounge slamming the door after him.

'What the hell is going on Suzanne?' Sam asked.

'I don't know.' I could feel hot tears welling up in my

eyes as she pulled me into a hug.

'All I know is he was a complete stranger but possessed many of the characteristics of Joseph,' I told Sam.

My blood ran cold as it dawned on me, *'Maybe I hadn't seen the full potential of Joseph yet!'*

After Sam and I had viewed all the photographs and had the time had flown by and Chris still hadn't shown up!

'John thinks all this Joseph stuff is a load of crap you know, so he won't be here tonight,' said Sam. *'No surprise there,'* I thought to myself. She went on to tell me that most of the others couldn't make it due to all sorts of genuine reasons. It was good that at least they let me know. She did say that Chris had just sent a text message saying he would be about half an hour.

I told Sam that I needed a smoke and had to get some things from my car and a minute later was enjoying the nicotine hit that all us smokers need. 'I must pack these in,' I said out loud, on feeling the cold night air and smoke hit my lungs giving them a double whammy.

It was really dark outside. The streetlights weren't brilliant and the majority of the light came from the Black Horse pub across the road. To my right, between the two pubs, standing back away from the road stood St. Nicholas church. I had never really noticed it before but standing silently in darkness, the old building held a kind of foreboding. Somehow I knew I had a connection with this ancient place of worship and burial.

I stubbed out the remains of my cigarette and went to my car, unlocked the boot and took out the box of incense I'd come for. I stepped back to close the boot and it suddenly slammed shut before I touched it. The shock made me drop the box of incense and lighter. The boot had closed so forcefully I didn't think the wind could be blamed.

On returning to the lounge I told Sam about how the car boot incident had nearly taken my face off. 'My God,' responded Sam.

It was at this point I decided to tell Sam about the events that had occurred at home on the Friday night. She just sat listening in silence, her mouth open and her eyes filled with tears as she heard the whole story.

When I'd finished she was just about to say something when Chris came in panting and breathless.

'I'm so sorry I'm late.' He had his hands in his pockets. The red shirt he was wearing was slightly damp around the collar and his blonde hair was dripping wet from the rain. He sat down and was rocking on the chair telling me what he had done in the pub over the weekend. 'I just can't rest, something is making me want to get the little girl out of this place. Can you please try and connect with her tonight Suzanne?' he asked.

'Yes of course, I need to know more myself.' The three of us continued discussing contact with the little girl.

Soon it was closing time and while Sam set about locking the pub up for the night, Chris leaned closer and told me he was being paralysed in his bed at night. He was also hearing voices coming from a corner of his bedroom but they were too quiet to understand. When he tried to sleep, he either got paralysed or his bed would rock. I knew exactly what he was going through and I told him of the things I'd experienced on that Friday night.

I had a horrible feeling in the pit of my stomach it wasn't just me Joseph was hurting. It was everyone involved as well. *Am I dragging everyone into danger*? I was undecided about carrying on the investigation. We chatted for a while about events over the last week. Chris need some advice so I told him to smoke smudge his bedroom and say healing prayers.

20TH SEPTEMBER INTIMIDATION

Smoke Smudging is an old Native American ceremony in which you burn sacred plants, such as sage, allowing the smoke to purify and bless a space'What a week it's been,' said Sam letting let out a sigh as she sank lower into the chair resting her head. I nodded in agreement at her comment.

'You're right there!' I nodded with a smile. I didn't know where the last week had gone. Sam quickly jumped up with a shocked expression on her face, leaning forward from her slouched position.

'Eeee. Chris, did Suzanne tell you about the freaky man that came into the bar around teatime tonight?'

He looked at us both confused, 'No?' he said in a curious manner.

'Well...' Sam said, 'Wait till you hear this!' Sam went on to tell Chris about the threatening behaviour and the way he seemed to know what was happening here in the pub. As I listened for a while to Sam's story, I could feel myself drifting away from the conversation to think of other ways I could be one step ahead of Joseph. I jumped as I felt a warmth on my hand and realized Chris was holding my right hand and gently squeezing it. He had a worried look on his face and was looking pale and haggard. I stared into his deep blue eyes, I could feel his pain and exhaustion.

'Are you okay?' he asked with a hesitant tone in his voice, 'Do you really want to go through with this after all of the threats?' He braced himself expecting me to say I didn't want to, but I knew in my heart I had no other choice. 'When my eyes met the little girl at the top of the stairs last Wednesday, I knew in my heart I had to help set her little soul free no matter what Joseph threw at me, whether it be threats and distractions or anything else I came across along the way,' I said. 'I have to let this little soul find her way home.' I looked back at them and saw both nodding in agreement.

Sam said, 'I have seen you change since last Wednesday, you look worn out Suzanne, it's strange how we all seem connected to this. It's been one hell of a week for us all.' Chris nodded again in agreement then replied.

'Okay Suzanne, if you're up for it, let's go upstairs and get some work done, we are running out of time.'

As Chris walked briskly to the staircase, I smiled at him then grabbed my things and followed. I could sense his determination. Sam began turning on the lights for the stairs and landing.

Climbing the stairs with my bag over my shoulder I approached the landing where I first saw the little girl pleading for help. A part of me wanted her to appear and communicate with me, but the other half hoped the pub would remain still and quiet.

We walked along the corridor, passing the ladies' toilets then the Gents, noticing the red patterned carpet in contrast against the cream paint. I ran my fingers along the wall feeling the pattern of the wallpaper. Although it had been painted over I could still feel every bump and groove of the pattern as I continued towards the white door at the end of the corridor. Entering the darkened room I couldn't see a thing. I stumbled up three stairs. I had to hold the wall to keep my balance. I saw the outline of a tall figure in front of me. It was Chris standing in the inner doorway. I could hear Sam talking.

'Where is the bloody light switch? She asked in a tense voice, 'I can't see a thing in this room.'

Oh my God! I thought to myself as I began to feel a draft coming from the room, it was freezing and the noise of the howling wind echoed around my head. I zipped up my coat against the freezing atmosphere that filled the room. I stepped closer towards Chris, standing to the left of the open doorway. I was reluctant to take another step further. Sam eventually found the light switch. I closed my eyes to protect them from the harsh bright light then slowly opened them to see a huge gaping hole to the left of the fire breast wall.

Everywhere was covered with a white dust. Bricks and rubble were scattered all over the floor. The dust even hung like a white mist in the air as we entered the room. The room temperature seemed as if it had dropped below zero. It was becoming so cold I found it difficult to breathe.

Chris signalled he was ready to start and grabbed a hammer and chisel out of his Reebok bag. Sam suggested she could clear a space for any rubble. I set about trying to connect to the little girl to see if we were getting close to where her body had been hidden. I backed away towards the settee under the windows at the far end of the room.

A few moments after closing my eyes a vision started to form.

I was outside in the back yard of the pub on cobbled stones. To my right I could make out the back entrance of the Wheatsheaf which led to the passageway connecting the bar and lounge. It was pitch black; my heart was beating harder as I walked into the shadow of the building. I didn't really want to enter, but a strange force was pulling me inwards. My chest was hurting and my breathing became heavier, I was screaming inside. I could see someone standing ahead of me. I was just able to make out a wooden door. Suddenly the door began to open, creaking sounds came from weathered hinges. The light from inside illuminated four or five figures. I could hear their boots scraping on the cobbles as they came towards me.

'You are not welcome here anymore,' came a man's voice, my heart was pounding out of my chest. 'We don't want you here' said another voice. They came marching in my direction forcing someone out of the pub into the alleyway, I stood watching. They couldn't see me. At the centre of this moving mayhem a large man was receiving many punches and kicks. 'You'll regret this night... AARGH! All of you will pay for this!' cried the man. As the vision faded, I stood transfixed with what I had just witnessed.

A large hand suddenly grabbed me by the throat, turned me around and pinned me against the pub wall. I was face to face with Joseph! His rancid breath clung to my skin as he spat a threat into my face.

'Remember what you saw them do to me 'cos I will never forget it'. His grip tightened on my throat and I thought I was going to pass out. 'I'll make sure you won't forget me, ever'.

Closing my eyes, I asked my spirit guides for help.

'Help me please, help me fight this wicked evil that is trying to kill me, please protect me and the people who are helping me.'

Joseph disappeared and I was back in the room with Sam and Chris.

'Are you okay?' Sam asked she was holding a bag of rubble. I looked at them both, 'Not really,' I replied quietly with tears starting to roll down my cheeks. Sam dropped the bag and came running towards me. Chris threw down his hammer and followed Sam.

She put her arms around me and I laid my head on her shoulder. Chris said, 'We could see that your body was in the room with us but your mind was somewhere else. Did you connect with the little girl.'

'No! But I met Joseph,' I answered sharply, my nerves were still jangling from my ordeal outside.

Chris said the child should be allowed to find peace and

20TH SEPTEMBER INTIMIDATION

I agreed with him, but Sam said 'Maybe we should leave this digging for tomorrow night? Let's have a break and warm up.'

After we'd all warmed through and had a short break, we decided to continue for a little while longer. The three of us climbed the stairs and resumed the search for any clues to the whereabouts of the little girl.

Chris began chiselling away at the bricks while Sam and I cleared the rubble that was piling up.

My mind was filled with doubts. *What if all this was a waste of everybody's time and effort. After all this digging, what if we find no trace of her in the wall*?

Chris said his arms were aching and needed a rest. Sam offered to take over. She agreed to remove one brick at a time as per Chris's instructions but as soon as she held the hammer and chisel she turned into a mad woman once more. She pounded relentlessly. I became worried that she could bring the whole structure down with her rage.

While Sam hacked mercilessly at the wall, Chris and I sieved through the rubble looking for anything that could be a clue.

I mentally asked for a sign of our progress. A voice answered, 'Every brick that is removed takes you closer to the truth.'

Sam began to slow her pace and dropped the hammer. She was breathless and covered in dust.

'Eeh! she said it's 3 am, I can't believe it's so late, we've been in this freezing cold room for over three hours.' Chris said we should call it a night. I could see we were all freezing. Sam sat down beside me trying to catch her breath.

'My God,' she said. 'My hands are a mess!' holding out her hands, 'Look they're a lovely colour, blue and grey.'

What with the wind blowing down the chimney and our digging, the room had become filled with a choking cloud of dust.

'Come on then, let's call it a night,' said Sam. Sensing my disappointment she started to rub my back as a gesture of comfort. 'It's fine Suzanne, we'll keep on digging. We haven't given up yet.'

I led the way along the corridor with Chris and Sam following behind turning off lights and closing doors.

'I think we make a good demolition team,' said Sam as she tried to lighten up our mood. The disappointment of not finding anything was sitting heavy upon all of us. As I was approaching the doorway to the gent's toilets, something ahead made me stop dead. Chris who was one step behind me bumped straight into me.

'What's the matter?' he asked in a quiet voice.

'Shhh, be quiet and stay perfectly still.' 'What's up Suzanne?' whispered Sam. 'I've just seen a man standing at the top of the landing,' I said looking at Chris and Sam. A grey tall shape was leaning against the wall. I could feel him glaring at me. Another figure emerged near to the men's toilets and stood only about two feet away from us. I was panicking, thinking, *what am I going to do*? This one was even taller than Joseph. He was wearing a black coat down to his thigh, he was really thin almost skeletal. His gaunt features made him look very menacing. He carried the marks of many fights on his face. The name Patrick came into my mind.

Standing next to him was a short tubby man with a round face and piggy little eyes. Instinctively I knew the two were Joseph's henchmen. The taller man had moved even closer. I could smell rotting flesh on his breath as he was exhaling. Suddenly he stepped to one side revealing a dark shape forming behind him.

20TH SEPTEMBER INTIMIDATION

There standing less than six feet away from me stood Joseph!

Dressed in a white shirt, grey waistcoat and trousers, his massive frame almost filled the corridor as he leaned forward to stare intently at me. I looked in horror as his repugnant face came even closer. He was like a huge cat playing with a tiny mouse. He was feeding on my terror. Relishing the taste of my fear. Our eyes were locked together. His thoughts were becoming mine. A bitter coldness enveloped my body as he stood just inches away. I found it hard to breathe.

'I'm going to have your mind, body and soul,' he gloated as I felt a numbing coldness tighten around my throat.

I wanted to say I wasn't scared of his threats but my whole being, even my thoughts were frozen.

'I will take you when I please, when the time is right. Until then, I will sip and savour your fear as if it were a fine wine. Go now and enjoy the time you have left that I am allowing you'.

An immense force hit my body and knocked me backwards into Chris standing behind. The corridor ahead stood empty.

The cold rapidly vanished and the three of us ran downstairs into the lounge without even a glance behind.

Sitting in the lounge, Sam and Chris had lots of questions because all they could see, was me reacting to things that were invisible to them. After I'd given them a full account of the meeting upstairs they were dumbfounded. 'I want to go home,' I told them both.

'Me too,' said Sam. 'Could you wait ten minutes while Chris and I lock up, then we can all leave together?'

'Thank God this night's coming to an end,' Sam said wearily

I felt glad to be going home soon, I knew Mark would be waiting for me. We made arrangements to meet the following morning and said our goodbyes.

I could barely keep my eyes open on the drive back home. Rolling down the passenger window, I hoped the cold fresh air coming into the car would keep me awake.

By some miracle, I managed to make it home without falling asleep at the wheel of my car whilst driving. Outside my house, I just there, feeling as if I'd fought ten rounds with Mike Tyson. I was utterly exhausted. My legs and shoulders ached from all the digging and coldness of that room. My face and hair were caked in brick dust and my brain was buzzing from all the madness. I felt so lost and afraid. I decided I needed a long soak in a hot bath, but before I dragged my weary body into the house, I begged for guidance.

A voice whispered gently inside. 'You have the strength. Your belief will carry you. Remember, every being has a weakness.

I stepped out of the car into a howling gale. I was halfway to the front door when I saw Mark step into the wind and start running towards me. Tears were streaming down my face as we met and he threw his arms around me. For the first time in many hours, I felt safe.

After enjoying a long soak I dried myself off and went to the kitchen. Mark had prepared a delicious breakfast which I ate hungrily. Once I'd downed my third cup of tea, Mark sat down opposite me with an expression on his face that meant he wasn't happy.

'I'll get this off my chest now Suzanne. I'm bloody furious with you. I've been ringing your mobile but it just goes to voicemail. I've been worried sick. Why didn't you call?'

'I'm sorry love', I replied feeling guilty. He was right

of course. I could have, and should have called him. The Wheatsheaf events had distracted me from doing the right thing and it was now affecting Mark as well.

The sadness filling Mark's eyes made me ache inside. 'I am truly sorry Mark,' I said reaching across the table to grasp his hand.

21st September
A Visit from The Canadians

A good night's sleep was what I really needed, but didn't get. My attempt at a quick power nap was disturbed with dreams of dead children, evil laughter, clawing hands reaching out for me, and of course, the grinning face of Joseph. I woke up more tired than when I'd crawled into bed an hour earlier.

The clock showed 7. 30 am as I rolled my weary body out of bed.

The kitchen floor was covered in clothes that I'd dragged from the spin drier in my frantic search for Francesca's school uniform. I looked around at the mess I had created and cursed silently under my breath.

I hated being disorganized and over the last few days the house seemed in total chaos. Perhaps this was one of the reasons for my change of personality. The gap between Mark and I was growing, and I found myself losing patience with him and the kids frequently. My mind was filled with The Wheatsheaf and it's collection of unearthly strangeness, and an anger bubbling away inside of me was fuelled with frustration and fear.

Joseph seemed hell bent on preventing me from finding the little girl, but why? Did he really believe I could take her to a place of peace? Remove her from his foul clutches?

21ST SEPTEMBER A VISIT FROM THE CANADIANS

If he thought it was possible then that gave me strength to continue.

I'd been lost in my thoughts so much I hadn't realised that I'd managed to clear all the clothes from the floor and fold them into a neat pile. I then set about preparing the breakfast table knowing full well it was yet another distraction I was using. As everything was ready to serve, the kitchen door burst open and a bleary-eyed Francesca stood in the doorway rubbing her eyes. 'Is brekky ready Mummy? I'm starving', she asked. 'Yes pet, but it will cost you one cuddle', I replied. She smiled broadly and ran from the doorway into my waiting arms. The closeness of this sleepy little person filled me with more warmth than any open fire could generate. *'If only life was as genuine and pure, everything would be wonderful,'* I thought to myself.

'You have a funny look on your face Mummy. Are you alright?' she enquired. I had momentarily slipped back into thoughts about the other little girl. 'I was just thinking how lucky I am to have such a lovely daughter.' I said masking the real reason. 'Right, what do want to eat love.' 'Can I make some Coco Pops please. I'll do it, 'cos I'm a big girl now.' she insisted. As I made myself a cup of tea I watched her get herself a bowl and spoon then carry the cereal packet to the table. I sat drinking my tea while she opened the box and began pouring. The portion was about twice as much as I would have given her, but she managed to eat the lot.

Francesca was putting her bowl and spoon into the dishwasher as Mark entered the kitchen carrying Alex. 'He needs changing before he has his breakfast,' Mark said moodily as he, handed Alex to me. 'I'll sort him out,' I responded sharply as he landed into my arms. He'd gained weight and weighed quite heavily in my arms. I grabbed his nappies and clothes for the day and made my way to the bathroom to clean him up.

A squeaky clean little boy was returned to Mark who began feeding Alex the breakfast he'd just prepared. Mark was about to feed Alex the last mouthful of porridge when I offered to make a cup of tea. 'Never mind the tea, we need to talk,' said Mark abruptly. 'Ok, no need to be so snappy,' I said.

We sat for several minutes discussing the problems we found ourselves facing. Mark accused me of ignoring him and neglecting the kids. I countered his argument by pointing out I'd been the main childminder in our relationship since the kids were born and it was about time he took over for a while. He couldn't come to terms with the need I had to bring some sort of resolve to the Wheatsheaf situation. We ended up going round in circles with neither of us reaching an agreement. I broke the stalemate by announcing it was time to take Francesca to school. Mark looked relieved that the conversation had ended.

Opening the front door I called to Mark 'After I drop Fran off at school I'm going to the library, but I should be back about 2.30 pm, is that alright?'. 'I suppose it'll have to be,' Mark grunted as he emerged from the kitchen carrying Alex. 'Bring some bread and milk in will you?' he asked. 'Ok,' I confirmed, then took Francesca's hand and left the house.

As we walked to the car a howling wind was trying it's best to knock us off our feet. I heard a distressed cry from Fran and looked to see that her scarf had managed to tangle itself around her head. I fixed the scarf dilemma and ran her the rest of the way to the car.

In the car, sheltered from the wind, I looked at myself using the rearview mirror. Windswept and interesting could've described my appearance.

21ST SEPTEMBER A VISIT FROM THE CANADIANS

'What a sight', I said out loud. 'Of course you are mum,' she laughed, 'but I still love you.' I hugged her closely.

When we arrived at the school gates, they were still open, which indicated that my furious driving had got us there in time. I quickly got Francesca's school stuff out of the boot, gave her kiss and watched as she sprinted through the main gates.

Driving towards Boldon the hollow feeling in my stomach told me I needed food. Fortunately, I knew of a place en route that did terrific hot sandwiches so in a short time I found myself in a queue of other hungry people. It was all so beautifully normal, a couple of lads in front talking about football, a man and woman bragging to another lady in the line about a cruise they'd just been on, and the staff behind the counter full of banter and cheeriness for their customers. So different to the things I'd experienced in the Wheatsheaf over the last few days. It refreshed me just listening to it all.

Carrying a hot bacon sandwich and a cup of tea I left the shop and was about to climb into my car when I heard someone shout my name. I turned to see Chris walking towards me.

'I was just walking to the Wheatsheaf can I jump in with you?' he asked. 'Come on, get in but hold my tea and bacon butty while I drive,' I replied. It was only a five-minute drive from the sandwich shop to our destination and when we arrived at the pub, Sam's car was nowhere to be seen. Both the tea and bacon sandwich were still hot enough to be really enjoyable so I opened my goodies and began savouring each tasty mouthful.

When I'd finished eating Chris asked, 'Do you want to wait inside, I've got a spare set of keys?' 'Try calling her mobile first,' I suggested. After a brief conversation with

HIDDEN EYES

Sam, Chris was able to tell me she was on her way. I locked the car and we walked to the main door. While Chris was busy opening up and turning off the internal alarm, I stood outside and looked around trying to picture how this area would have looked at the turn of the 1900's. What a different place it would have been. A much harder, basic, and more demanding way of life than perhaps we could tolerate nowadays.

My daydream of bygone times in Boldon was shattered by Chris shouting 'Bloody hell Suzanne, come and have a look at this!'. I walked into the bar and saw what had caused Chris to shout. Everywhere was covered in a thin layer of grey cement dust and soot. It appeared that the mess had come down the chimney because several bricks were lying in the hearth. 'Can you give me a hand sorting this out Suzanne? Phil will give me my P45 if he sees this mess.' I told Chris that I would clean the tables and bar if he blocked up the fireplace and hoovered the carpet. Nearly twenty minutes later and sweating like pigs we had the place looking normal again.

'I think we've earned a brew Suzanne, don't you?' I gave Chris the thumbs up to his suggestion and off he went to make the tea.

While I'd been cleaning the bar I spotted a door with small panes of glass that I'd never noticed before. Now standing alone in the bar waiting for my tea, I once again looked over to that door. I was strangely drawn to it. I went over and peeped in through one of the grubby panes. I found I was looking into the office where the black spiral staircase had been when it was Joseph's office.

'Here ya are, get this down yer neck,' said Chris carrying two steaming hot cups of tea into the bar. I was itching to find out what caused all the dust so I said to Chris, 'Do you mind if I take mine upstairs? I want to see

21ST SEPTEMBER A VISIT FROM THE CANADIANS

what caused all this mess.' He told me that he still had some cleaning to do in the lounge, so couldn't come with me.

I got to the room we had been working in the night before and slowly opened the door. 'Oh my God,' I uttered out loud. The hole in the fireplace wall was about half as big again as when we left it. Newly removed bricks were strewn around at the base of the wall and a fresh layer of dust was covering everything in the room. There were some partly removed bricks hanging from the hole. Something had been clawing at the loose brickwork. It was only as I got further into the room I began to see them... . several small footprints leading to the wall. Looking closer at the bricks I could see small hand prints in the dust. She'd been here. She was showing me I was in the right place! My determination to make the connection with her grew stronger.

I returned to the bar and told Chris of my findings. He grabbed a couple of soft drinks and ushered me over to a table eager for more details. I sat with him describing what I found.

Suddenly there was a loud BANG, BANG, BANG on the window. I nearly jumped off the seat. I looked over to the source of the noise and saw Sam looking through the window and waving. Beside her stood Denise. By the time my heart rate had settled down, the two of them were inside the pub. We greeted each other warmly. Chris offered them a cup of tea and of course I couldn't let them drink alone so added to the order as well.

We sat there drinking our teas and I listened as Sam told Denise about the weird man who started picking on me in the lounge the previous day. 'You don't half attract them Suzanne, if he shows up again I'm calling the Police,' said Sam. I could tell she wasn't joking.

Denise looked at me with sympathy, 'I can't imagine what it must be like for you. You look absolutely knackered. We can try to support you but basically, all we can do is watch while you face these things alone. She was right. Only I could actually see most of what was going on. All I could do was tell those about me what I was seeing. That fact didn't make me feel any stronger.

'Have you thought about what we should do next in finding the girl?' asked Sam. 'There must be something upstairs to help me make a connection with her,' I replied, 'but I also have to think about this guy Joseph. It looks like he's trying frighten us away and stop me getting near her. Actually talking it through with my three friends made me realise how vulnerable my position was. Feeling dead on my feet didn't help either.

It was really enjoyable sharing all the banter as we waited for Phil to arrive and start the first shift of the day. Then it happened, just a small movement out of the corner of my eye. It brought my attention to the door with the small glass panes.

Could I make out a shadow there? No, it was something the other side of the door I could see. Something moving from side to side. Something trying to attract my attention.

I watched with tension building inside of me. Suddenly a face, hideously distorted as it pressed against the glass, stared right at me.

It was Joseph! Even though his features were contorted through the glass, I could see he was relishing my unease, an unease that must have showed on my face.

'Suzanne, are you ok?' Chris asked. 'Joseph is looking at me through that door by the bar,' I replied. Everyone at the table turned their eyes to where I was looking. 'Sorry Suzanne, I can't see anything,' said Sam. Chris agreed with her, but Denise didn't utter a word, I knew she could sense

21ST SEPTEMBER A VISIT FROM THE CANADIANS

his presence.

Bang! We all jumped. Sam screamed and Chris was out of his seat ready for a fight. Phil came walking into the bar laughing. He'd seen us all staring at the door where I'd seen Joseph and realized we didn't know he was there. 'I bet you all thought that was Joseph knocking on the bar?', Phil said still smirking from his practical joke. After hanging his coat up, Phil joined us briefly for a catch- up.

'Oh ha ha!' Sam laughed, 'Don't you dare do that again, I nearly crapped myself. She reached over to smack him on the head. .

'So let's hear what's been happening since I saw you last, Suzanne?' said Phil. After hearing all the details he said, 'Why didn't you ring me, I would have been straight over, If anything happens like that again, let me know straight away'.

Chris pointed out we should be making a move to leave for the library. Time was tight for him, so we quickly arranged to spend only an hour checking records for the Wheatsheaf, and then grab some lunch and go over any notes we'd made. I was eager to find some history on the building and there might be some names in the 1901 census I could recognize. It felt like being on a school day trip, which lightened the mood slightly as we returned to our cars. Sam and Denise led the way in Sam's' black VW and I followed, not knowing the area as well as Sam.

Following Sam proved quite difficult because it was raining heavily and she was such a fast driver. At times, I think she forgot I had to follow her. On the way Chris mentioned the noises that were coming from the corner of his bedroom at night, 'I don't like it Suzanne, it's freaking me out, I can understand what you're going through,' he said. 'Do you think I'm connected in some way to the little girl? he asked.

'Maybe, you could have been at the pub in a past life.' I said, 'We'll talk more about it when we get back.'

We pulled into the library car park and saw Sam and Denise waiting for us. I parked up and the four of us ran through the rain into the main entrance. Sam went to the reception and made the necessary arrangements for us to carry out our research. On return she told us the archives were downstairs.

A pleasant young man took us to a section where he handed us three books entitled History of Boldon and covered all the years from the early 1870s - to the early 1900s. 'These are the books you need, please be careful with the pages as they are very old.' The young man smiled and left us to our research.'

We sat down, each of us holding a different book. As I turned the pages, I found lots of names and dates, some I could relate to. My eyes were taken to the headings and job titles; miner, son of a miner, carpenter, son of a carpenter. It was remarkable how many men followed their father's trade going down through the generations. I was deep in thought, soaking up the information when a hand touched my right shoulder. I jumped. You don't expect that in a quiet public library.

'Suzanne,' Chris whispered with a serious look on his face, 'Read this!' as he handed me a little red book. The title was, 'Finding of Bodies in a Manor House'. Chris pulled up a seat beside me. A quick scan of the book revealed it was a short vague story about a man named Joseph, who owned the Wheatsheaf pub in West Boldon and a manor house which was situated close to the pub. Apparently when Joseph was digging the garden one day, he uncovered the bodies of more than twenty women and children. The book stated that it was thought to be a burial ground from a battle that happened in that area. It was

21ST SEPTEMBER A VISIT FROM THE CANADIANS

written as if Joseph was some sort of celebrity because of his find. It made me so angry to read how the village had embraced this evil bastard of a man. 'What!' I said to Chris, 'how could this happen?'

'I don't know Suzanne, but it's looking like he had the village in the palm of his hand at one time in his life,' said Chris. 'He was a bully and a trickster,' I said angrily. Chris stood up shaking his head.

'He wanted people to think he was the local hero, it was a cover up to fool people, he needed everyone to think he was a good man.' He may have had some 'friends' in the local police or someone official to protect him. 'The plot thickens!' I said. I glanced over at Sam; she was busy writing down some names and notes.

'Did you find anything on the little girl?' I asked Sam. She looked at me and shook her head to say no. I looked over to Denise, she was reading information on the history of the pub.

Sam asked her, 'Have you found out anything yet?' 'A bit, but nothing about the little girl though.'

Time was running out fast, so we gathered our notes together, made arrangements for another visit to this section, and left.

It was with mixed feelings that I headed for my car. I found it so frustrating to read about Joseph being held in such high regard because of his find. My belief was that he was probably responsible for their deaths and disposal of the bodies, making his claim of finding them to avert any suspicion from himself. On the other hand I was delighted to have found proof of Joseph's existence and other details relevant to the pub.

Sam asked if we wanted to grab a sandwich in a local cafe that was renowned for its food. We readily agreed and ran to the high street, fighting the wind and rain. Like four drowned rats we arrived at the cafe and joined the queue inside.

Once served, we left carrying our bags of food. A return to the cars meant battling the elements again.

Chris climbed into my car and exclaimed, 'Oh God that wind takes your breath away and I'm soaked.' He slid into the seat, placed my handbag on the floor and put his lunch and paperwork on his lap. He was like a little child as he strapped himself in, balancing his food bag on his knee. He didn't say much to me on the drive back to the pub, I could tell he was trying to come to terms with the information we had just found in the library.

Back at the Wheatsheaf, the four of us huddled around a table in the bar and began to unwrap the food we'd bought. It wasn't long before we were all tucking in without conversation spoiling the moment. Once the last crumbs had been consumed discussions began about the notes we written.

I brought up the story about Joseph finding the bodies. 'Why didn't the locals or police question what was he digging for?

I don't think you need to dig over three foot deep usually. Was he trying to reach Australia?' For the life of me I couldn't think why a burial ground supposedly because of a battle, would only contain women and children.

Phil came over to the table with four mugs of tea and asked how we'd got on. 'I tell you what Phil, we have found out some really interesting information on Joseph,' Chris said enthusiastically. 'Well then?' Phil asked.

We filled him in on the information that came up for Joseph. Dates and names that we had found which coincided with the names I had picked up on over the past week were discussed. It confirmed more facts in this story

21ST SEPTEMBER A VISIT FROM THE CANADIANS

were correct and that I wasn't just making things up. Chris related his information from the little red book, about Joseph innocently digging in the garden one day finding a burial ground near the old manor house.

'I smell a rat in this story,' I commented, and everyone present nodded their head in agreement.

I asked Chris where the manor house was; he stood up and explained that it's opposite the traffic lights on the end of the road. I suggested we could take a little walk over to the house to see what I could discover. My friends thought this was a good idea. As we finished of our teas I asked if there had been other odd things happen in the past. Sam remembered the story of a previous landlord who tried to burn the bar down but the fire had mysteriously went out. It had all backfired on him because one of the bar staff told the brewery about his attempted arson.

Listening to that story gave me a feeling that Joseph had something to do with it and wondered whether he could have driven the landlord out of his mind.

As we sat sharing our thoughts about the little girl and Joseph, we hadn't noticed an elderly couple were standing, waiting to get someone's attention. Phil stood up and went over to find out what they wanted. Because they were too far away from us we couldn't make out what was being said. I could however, see that Phil had a strange look on his face and was nodding as the woman spoke. He turned and called over to us. 'These people are from Canada. They're on holiday here.

The lady is originally from Boldon and used to live here in the pub as a little girl. I've asked them to join us.' With that he led the couple over to our table where Sam shook hands with them and introduced everyone. The lady was called Kathleen and her husband was called Carl. Looking at them I estimated they must be in their eighties.

They were both well dressed and spoke with soft accents, similar to Americans but not as harsh.

'I hope you don't mind us intruding like this? But as we were passing in a taxi I spotted the Wheatsheaf and felt compelled to come and see the old place,' Kathleen said apologetically. Phil smiled at Kathleen and told her it was no problem, and that they were very welcome to have a look round if they wished. I could see Sam was bursting to ask a question. 'How long ago did you live here?' Kathleen looked at Sam and replied, 'My parents had this place in the 1930s. I was about five years old and my sister Janice was eight.'

I was also bursting with a hundred and one questions for Kathleen but let her tell the story of her childhood without prompting.

Kathleen continued, 'We lived upstairs, Janice had the bedroom at the top of the stairs and my room was next door to hers.'

The hairs on my arms began to rise.

'Janice always had trouble sleeping and was plagued with nightmares. She often reported seeing a little girl about her own age, appearing in her room at night. Janice often told our parents that the child had asked for help and cried. I think they thought she was making things up and didn't do anything about it. My sister and I carried troubled memories of living here for many years afterwards.'

Phil invited the couple to have a look round and Kathleen readily accepted. The first place she looked at was the office beside the bar. She opened the glass paned door and exclaimed, 'The spiral staircase has gone. That's made more room in here!'

We all entered the corridor next to the office as Kathleen led the group. About halfway along she pointed at the outside wall and said, 'I remember there was a door

21ST SEPTEMBER A VISIT FROM THE CANADIANS

here that leads to the yard outside.'

I glanced at Phil and Chris who both stood there opened mouthed. They were hearing facts that I'd told them several days ago being confirmed by this total stranger.

'Would you like to see the cellar?' asked Sam.

'NO!' she replied in a firm voice, 'I never liked it down there.' We all looked at each other in amazement.

'Did something bad happen there?' I asked. 'I remember helping my Dad decorate the bar for Christmas. We'd gone down into the cellar to get some boxes of tinsel that he'd stored there. Dad was lifting the boxes from a shelf and I was carrying them to the bottom of the cellar stairs. It felt really cold and gloomy. I heard breathing close to me. I knew it wasn't Dad because he was still over at the shelves and I was at the bottom of the stairs. Something really cold brushed against my legs then I felt an icy cold touch on my cheek. I just screamed and ran up the stairs to get away from whatever it was in the cellar. I never went back after that.' The fear still showed on Kathleen's face as she recalled the incident. 'Wow', was all Sam could say.

'Can we go and have a look upstairs?' asked Kathleen.

By this point I was mesmerised by this lady's stories, it was so fascinating to listen to her experiences. 'Yes of course,' said Phil, 'You lot go on while I look after the bar.'

The Canadian lady walked ahead pointing out various changes she noticed and recalling anecdotes about the pub. I listened with great interest and thought how remarkable she was, being able to remember her childhood memories as if they had happened just recently.

In the group following Kathleen and her husband, I took up the rear. It was captivating to hear her perspective of the rooms from the eyes of a child. Her family had lived at the pub for about two years and moved out when she was seven.

Sam asked her when she'd last been at the Wheatsheaf.

Kathleen replied, 'The day we moved out. I didn't want to see the place again until today'

'Oh my God,' Sam said, 'So how is everything so clear to you?' 'I don't know, I can't explain it?' She said. 'As we drove past the pub earlier on, I got a feeling in my heart, I had to come here again, we were on our way to visit family in Gateshead when I saw the pub.' Kathleen pointed out that the stairs and the landing hadn't changed and the windows at the top of the stairs were still the same as she remembered them. I sighed, thanking God for bringing this lady with her confirmation of names and events I'd mentioned. It was just what I had needed to strengthen the personal beliefs I held through visions and premonitions, it was uncanny but so welcome.

Upstairs we walked along the corridor. Kathleen entered the ladies toilets and exclaimed, 'My word, this room has changed so much, this was one big room.' I stood by the door and listened as she described the room, saying that there used to be two windows. She asked if the mirror pulled out. Sam found a latch and pulled it open to reveal an outer window. Kathleen said she often looked out of this window to watch people walking up and down the street. She remembered the church over the road and miners covered in dirt coming straight to the pub from work. She said that this had been her sisters room.

'I can remember there was a black fireplace and it was always cold in here,' she said rubbing her arms as her memory took her back to those bygone days.

'Janice would tell me about the little girl appearing, and a tall horrible man walking into the room. She sometimes saw him standing at the top of the landing as well so she

21ST SEPTEMBER A VISIT FROM THE CANADIANS

usually ended up sleeping in my room. She felt safer with me.

I asked if she heard or saw things, she replied, 'My sister used to hear a lot more than I did, maybe because she was a bit older? I don't know but I did hear voices whispering sometimes, and of course that time in the cellar. Our parents never believed us when we told them. They used to say we were imagining things.'

Every word Kathleen spoke was confirming lots of details I'd mentioned previously to Sam, Chris and Phil. Like pieces of a jigsaw fitting into place, my visions were being verified. I felt so relieved, like a weight had lifted from my shoulders.

Next, Kathleen had a look inside the gents toilets. Again her description of the room as she remembered it matched mine exactly.

She then led us down the corridor to where the storeroom and kitchen were. As she stood in front of the two doors she smiled at some unspoken memory then entered through the kitchen door.

'This is where my mum used to spend a lot of her time.' She described a big stove with shelves on the back wall and a large wooden table that stood in the centre of the room. She also remembered a fireplace and indicated where the spiral staircase used to be.'

We left the kitchen and entered the storeroom where we'd been knocking a hole in the chimney breast wall. The cold hit us like an Arctic blast.

'Are you having some repairs done in here?' Kathleen asked. I quickly took Sam to one side and whispered, 'We need to tell her what's going on.' Sam nodded, stepped forward and proceeded to provide the couple with a quick explanation.

'That's awesome,' she said, her voice quavering a little

at what Sam had said.

I chipped in, 'We haven't found her yet, but we think it's just a matter of time before we find some answers behind this wall.'

Sam smiled and suggested we all should go back downstairs. 'I will put the kettle on and make us a hot drink, it's too cold to stand about in this room.' Everyone agreed and the group made their way back downstairs.

We sat enjoying a warming brew that Sam had conjured up in record time and I found myself sat next to Kathleen. She asked if I was also one of the staff. I explained my connection and what I was hoping to achieve. Kathleen listened intently then said, 'I wish you the best of luck in finding what are you looking for.'

'Thank you,' I said with a smile, 'I cannot thank you enough for sharing the memories of your childhood. You have confirmed everything I'd mentioned from my psychic visions, and it has let me know that the information I have been given is correct. It was fate that brought you here today.' Everyone agreed with me.

Once we had all enjoyed Sam's warming brew it was time for Kathleen and Carl to bid us farewell. Sam called a local taxi firm and Kathleen left contact details with Sam. We all chatted together as we waited for their taxi to arrive. Kathleen said she was eager to know the outcome of our quest and Sam promised to keep her informed.

As the taxi pulled up outside the main door, Kathleen took my hand in hers and said, 'I will tell Janice about today, she will be very interested to hear about the little girl because she had more to do with her than I did.'

The Canadians climbed into the taxi and we stood waving goodbye until the vehicle drove out of sight. We then trooped back in for a final discussion.

'That was amazing!' said Chris. 'What a coincidence'.

21ST SEPTEMBER A VISIT FROM THE CANADIANS

It's more than a coincidence', said Denise. 'I think that was evidence that some greater powers are looking over us and lending a hand.'

'Oh MY God! Look at this Suzanne!' Sam handed me the piece of paper with Kathleen's details. It hadn't really dawned on me at the time, but Kathleen was one of the names I'd mentioned previously. I put my hand over my mouth, *were we closer to the little girl than we realised?*

'I feel there is a light at the end of the tunnel,' said Chris as he stood up to place the empty cups on the bar.

I looked at the bar clock and saw it was nearly time to collect Fran from school. Arrangements were made to return to the dig at about eight o'clock the following evening. I told Chris and Sam I was working at a psychic fair in Hartlepool and wouldn't be finished until 11.30 pm. 'No problem, Suzanne,' said Sam, 'We'll just keep going until you get here,' she answered.

My mobile started ringing in my bag. It was Mark.

Taking it out of my bag I saw there had been several missed calls from him. *I'd had the bloody thing on silent.*

'Hi love, you ok?' I said.

'What time are you coming home? Remember you have a daughter to pick up from school,' he said sarcastically.

'Mark, don't be like this, I am leaving now,' I replied.

'Don't be late!' he snapped. I didn't get a chance to reply. He just hung up. *Great*! I thought to myself. *Another lovely evening at home with Mark giving me the silent treatment.*

I just looked for a moment at the blank screen, shook my head then popped the phone back into my bag along with all the notes and things we'd been collating. I said goodbye to everyone and collected my car from the car park.

Getting to Fran's school on time and getting back home went without too much of a problem despite the continuing bad weather and once in the comfort of our warm little home everything seemed normal again.

Mark was sitting in his usual seat and raised a finger to his lips as we entered the lounge to indicate Alex was asleep. I crept over to look at my son sleeping peacefully. He looked so beautiful.

I went into the kitchen to make a meal and Mark followed me in. Mark looked at me and said, 'Let's forget all that Wheatsheaf crap for a bit, shall we go out for a meal?' That remark told me two things; One, Mark hadn't taken on board how important that 'Wheatsheaf crap' was to me, and Two, he was making some effort to be friends with me.

At least, on this occasion, I agreed with Mark. Perhaps doing something together as a family was what we needed.

With the kids dressed and ready, we set off for a new pub in Boldon called The Story Book. The meals were cheap and cheerful and there was a large play area for children. The food wasn't bad and Fran had a great time in the ball pool.

Back home, the evening rounded off with a family viewing of Barbie's Swan Lake. Not really suitable for adults but it was Fran's favourite. At bedtime she put up no resistance and slipped between her Hello Kitty bedsheets without a murmur. Within minutes she was sound asleep and there wasn't a peep out of her for the rest of the night.

Once I knew the kids were settled I decided to take a nice long soak in the bath to ease my aching limbs. Mark acting totally out of character said he would run the bath for me, and while he did that I went to the bedroom and slipped out of my clothes.

Sliding into that hot water was a pleasure I'd almost

21ST SEPTEMBER A VISIT FROM THE CANADIANS

forgotten existed. I let the sheer luxury of it, carry me off into a place where there was no Joseph, no Wheatsheaf, just blue skies and sunshine.

I laid like that with my eyes closed, until the bath water started to cool down. On opening my eyes I saw a strange mist starting to fill the bathroom. At first glance I thought it was just steam but no, this was something different. From where I lay it looked like it was coming out from the walls and ceiling. Any warmth in the room had vanished. I started to shiver uncontrollably and I was becoming very frightened. I tried calling Mark's name but no sound left my throat.

My lungs began to hurt as my breathing became quite laboured. My heart was beating rapidly. I could feel unseen hands touching my body. Probing and exploring. Suddenly something covered my face and pushed my head under the water. I tried to sit up but whatever it was held me firmly down. I managed to free my left arm and bang on the side of the bath to try and attract Mark's attention. I was starting to lose consciousness. I could hear Mark kicking at the bathroom door trying to get in. As suddenly as it started, everything weird stopped. My head flew from underneath the water and I sat coughing. In the same instance, the door burst open and Mark came tumbling into the bathroom.

I just laid in the cold water for several minutes. I felt violated and dirty. Mark knelt beside the bath trying to offer some words of comfort but no matter what he said didn't stop my pitiful sobbing.

I cried for myself, I cried for Fran and Alex, I cried for Mark, but mainly I cried because the realization hit me like an iron fist.

Joseph had just paid me a home visit.

22nd September
Breaking News

Sleep was an impossibility that night. How could I ? I had been assaulted, physically, sexually and mentally in my own bathroom!

Never mind sleep, I was scared to even close my eyes.

Afterwards Mark and I discussed the incident. He'd heard me banging and tried the door handle. Although I never lock the door when having a bath, somehow the door wouldn't open.

He'd pushed and kicked at it because he thought I'd been taken ill.

No matter how hard he had tried, the door wouldn't budge. Then suddenly it was open and he literally just fell through the door onto the floor inside the bathroom. I knew one thing, if he hadn't got in when he did, I would have probably drowned. I'd been seconds away from opening my mouth to take a breath. Not really the right thing to do when your head's underwater. After what we'd been through both of us settled for an early night in bed. Mark drifted off quite quickly but I just lay there turning events over in my mind. I was shaken about how close I'd come to drowning in my own bath.

Mark started mumbling in his sleep. I couldn't make out what he was saying but whatever it was, sounded very troubled. I realized he was holding my hand just like he had when kneeling beside the bath. I freed my hand from his and sat up. Dawn was just starting to break judging by the light coming through the bedroom curtains.

I put my dressing gown on and nervously stepped out onto the landing. I was very jumpy, listening to every groan and creak that houses normally make when everything is quiet. My own breathing was possibly the loudest noise I could hear at that moment. I crossed the landing and went to the toilet. As I came out of the toilet I stopped dead. There was the shape of a man standing in the bedroom doorway. My pulse started to speed up. Then he spoke, 'You Ok love?' said Mark stretching, and giving out a huge yawn.

'My throat feels like I have swallowed razor blades, I'm on my way downstairs for a hot drink,' I replied.

'Okay, put the kettle on and I will be two minutes,' he responded. I chose to wait for him coming out of the toilet rather than venturing downstairs alone.

I pulled back the landing curtains and looked out over the communal car park and fields beyond. The sun was just starting it's daily rise into the early morning sky. It seemed like nature was saying, *no matter what happens around you, elsewhere life just carries on.*

Mark led the way downstairs and went to the kitchen while I lit the fire in the lounge. After a few minutes, Mark entered carrying a tray of hot buttered toast and a pot of tea.

'What did you make of last night Mark?' I asked.

'Well to be honest, it scared the shit out of me, I heard banging and thought it was Fran running round. I looked in on her but she was out for the count. Then I realized the banging was coming from the bathroom. I knew you were in there so I tried to get in but the door wouldn't open, it was then I started kicking at it. Next thing, the door burst open and I couldn't stop myself from flying through into the bathroom and falling on the floor. All I saw was you starting to sit up, coughing and crying. What the hell is that all about Suzanne?'

I explained to Mark that I believed Joseph had somehow managed to attach himself to me and was now in the house.

'What can you do about that?' he asked with a very worried look on his face.

'I don't have a clue at present,' I answered honestly.

There didn't seem to be any more we could add to that subject so I sat just picking at a slice of toast. It was hardly surprising that my appetite wasn't at it's best that morning.

I let my mind wander and began thinking of what the day ahead had on offer. The kids had to be sorted out. Fran had to be taken to school. There was the usual housework and I had that psychic fair to attend in Hartlepool at 6 pm.

Mark said, 'I'll get Francesca up if you would take care of Alex this morning? I accepted his suggestion and went upstairs to Alex's bedroom.

'Good morning Sunshine,' I smiled. He giggled and his little face lit up with a big wide smile as I bent over his cot to pick him up. He opened his arms to ask for a carry. As I held my baby son tears were once more running down my face. Thoughts of what happened last night came rushing back to me. I was grateful for the family I had and knew I had to be strong for them.

I spent the next hour washing and changing Alex, giving him his breakfast and noticing how much Alex had grown recently. He had put on so much weight. He loved his food... a really healthy little boy.

By that time Fran was ready for school. Mark said he would walk her to the school gates. He put Alex into his warm coat and mittens then strapped him into the

22ND SEPTEMBER BREAKING NEWS

pushchair. As they said goodbye, the house became very quiet. My eyes felt so sore and heavy. I laid down on the couch and used the cushions as pillows. I was looking at the TV but not actually watching it. I must have drifted off because then next thing I was aware of was something cold and wet touching my face. I sat bolt upright with shock only to see Alex clinging to the side of the couch and giggling over his dummy at me.

I smiled with equal measures of relief and joy at what I saw. Scooping him up I placed him on my knee, pleased it was nothing sinister that had woken me. I sat rocking him in my arms whilst singing a lullaby and he quickly fell asleep, allowing me the opportunity to continue my conversation with Mark. I found him in the dining room, sitting reading his newspaper.

He put down his paper as I entered the room and looked up at me. There was an awkwardness between us that had never been there before.

'Are you going to that Wheatsheaf place again today?' he demanded to know.

'I promised I would help them after the fair tonight,' I replied. 'So another late night is it?' he sneered.

'Please Mark stop being like this, I have to see it through, can't you understand?'

'All I understand is, you'll do what you want and sod everything else,' he sighed.

'I don't want us to keep arguing, I need your support,' I responded.

'I wish you had never got involved in the first place,' he snapped and that was the end of the matter.

With the argument put aside we decided a trip to the local supermarket was necessary as we were running low on a few items of food. The next couple of hours were spent stocking up on what we needed to the

HIDDEN EYES

accompaniment of Alex wailing his head off through teething.

It was a blessing to finish the shopping and make our way home.

Mark offered to collect Fran from school. I think he did it to avoid talking to me. Things were getting that bad between us.

'I'll be about half an hour,' he shouted, slammed the front door, and was gone.

Alex and I shared some quality mother and baby time playing together. It was so nice doing 'normal things' that 'normal' mothers did, but even as I held my baby, deep down, my instincts told me it couldn't last.

I heard the front door open and moments later Francesca came dashing into the lounge. She could hardly contain her excitement as she blurted out, 'I've been picked to be Mary in the Christmas play.'

'Wow, that's great Fran,' I said encouragingly.

'Yeah, but that Lewis Thompson is going to be Joseph,! He's horrible and always picks on me.' She said.

'Never mind love, I bet it will be alright.' I said trying to reassure her.

'Ted Jenkins should play Joseph, 'cos he's cute and has ginger hair,' she said justifying her dislike of the boy called Lewis.

Mark helped me prepare tea and we sat around the dining room table quietly eating. Fran was still going on about the Christmas play but very little conversation passed between Mark and I. Once everyone had finished eating I told Mark that I had to get ready for the evening fair. He said he would tidy up the tea things and I went upstairs to prepare for the night's work ahead.

I emerged from the bedroom like most women do, full makeup, good gear on, and looking like a different person.

22ND SEPTEMBER BREAKING NEWS

I said my farewells to Mark and the kids then drove off in the direction of Hartlepool.

The traffic was getting heavier as I neared the town, road works were causing bumper to bumper hold ups. I checked the time and became anxious about being late. I rang the organiser but it just went to her voicemail, so I left a message telling her I was on my way.

Arriving at the venue I saw that a queue had already formed and by the number of people waiting, it looked like the evening was going to be busy.

I parked up and squeezed through the waiting crowd to reach the main entrance. Inside the building, I reported to Helen the organiser. She smiled broadly when she saw me. I was shown to my table and I quickly set it out with all my little bit and bobs that I usually displayed and took my seat waiting for my first client.

Half an hour passed and most of the other readers were on their first or second client. Nobody had come to my table. I felt invisible.

For some reason, my table held no attraction to the public that night. I sat there shuffling my tarot pack watching the other readers busy with clients, and wondered what was wrong with me.

After two hours I decided to go to the bar for a drink. It couldn't do any harm because nobody wanted me. A soft drink eased my sore throat and I felt able to take my seat behind my table once more.

There were only two people who came to me for readings before the event closed. Both were delighted with the content and went away very happy. I packed my bags and said goodnight to everyone. There was only one thing on my mind. The Wheatsheaf!

I couldn't wait to meet up with Sam and the others again, even though it filled me with fear just thinking about it. The A19 was the quickest route and I headed north towards Boldon whilst keeping just within the legal speed limits.

I jumped with surprise as my mobile phone buzzed to indicate a text message had been received. Keeping my eyes on the road I fumbled in my handbag and grabbed my phone.

Checking the screen I saw a short message from Sam.

The words nearly burst my brain. I could hardly believe what I was reading. Talk about breaking news... .

There, on that small screen before me, was displayed the stark message. 'We have found her!!!'

I let out a shriek and punched the air. I almost lost control of the car but rapidly came back down to earth before any danger was caused. Tears were running down my cheeks. I couldn't believe it.

From that point, the drive to Boldon was just a blur. I was aware that some other motorists on the A19 found my driving somewhat annoying, judging by the number of lights flashing and horns beeping as I drove north.

I arrived at the Wheatsheaf and abandoned my car in the car park. I wasn't sure if I'd locked it, but at that moment in time I didn't care.

The main door to the lounge was still open and I entered running, up the stairs as fast as my legs could carry me. Making my way along the upstairs corridor, my excitement was growing. I made a most dramatic entrance into the room where Sam and the others were working.

The hole was huge. Chris was standing beside it covered from head to foot in cement dust. He stood like a grey ghost holding something towards me. It took me a moment to adjust to the awful cold in the room. I looked at what he was offering me.

'I found this behind the wall Suzanne,' he said.

There, in his hand were the remains of a girl's shoe. You could clearly identify the heel and strap despite the ravages of time. The item looked very fragile but convinced me she'd been behind that wall.

I took them from him. The remnants of that small shoe filled me with so much emotion I started to cry. I looked at her shoe. That poor child whose life had been dominated by Joseph. It was too painful to contemplate. As I stood there sobbing Sam came over to me and placed a blanket around my shoulders. She hugged me close and whispered, 'You were right.' Denise stepped forward and put her hand on my shoulder. 'Well done,' was all she needed to say. I wanted an excuse to take a break for a moment just to clear my head so I suggested getting drinks for the team.

Denise's son Stephen offered to accompany me to the loungeto help me.

I waited while Stephen took everyone's orders and we were about to leave the room when two stacked barstools in the corner of the room started wobbling.

'What's wrong?' said Stephen.

'Shh!', I cautioned and pointed to the barstools.

He gripped my right shoulder and watched as one of the barstools rose from its position, fly through the air, and smash to pieces on the wall beside where we stood.

I could see Stephen was trembling. The noise caused Sam to run to where we stood. 'Are you ok?' she asked with some urgency.

'No, this is really starting to get dangerous,' I told her picking up the broken pieces of the stool. 'From now on nobody is to be left alone. Even if you need the toilet, someone goes with you, right!'. I pointed out that didn't include me because I had things to prepare if I was to help the child. After much protesting everyone accepted why I needed to be the exception. As to their need not to be alone,

I didn't have to say much more to convince our little band of workers, that I was giving good advice.

It was so cold in the room where we were working, the need for heat became essential. As a group we agreed to go down to the lounge for a break and get some warmth into our bodies.

When the pub was closed, the lounge always felt strangely silent. It could have had something to do with the area by the DJ's box I'd named Joseph's corner. I quickly replenished the salt around our safe area and we sat waiting while Sam and Denise went away to prepare some hot drinks. I sat quietly with my eyes closed, praying for guidance. The answer came back that I should remain strong, use the knowledge I'd built up over the years, and believe that the Lord would carry me through adversity.

I began to formulate a plan in my mind on how to deal with Joseph.

When Sam and Denise returned with the hot drinks, I announced that I had to face Joseph alone. He needed to be shown I could stand up to him no matter how difficult that task may be. Sam tried to change my mind and Chris also thought it was madness, but my explanation was reluctantly accepted by the group.

When I felt ready I spoke up and said, 'Is everyone ok?'. The nodding heads gave me my answer. 'Right, let's get on with it,' I said, collected a small bag of crystals from my handbag, and stepped out of the safe zone. There was only the light above the table where my friends were sat that provided any illumination for the room so the further I moved away, the darker it became.

'Come on Joseph, here I am,' I bellowed as loud as I could muster. Nothing happened. I waited a minute or so and shouted, 'Where are you, Joseph?'. Again there was silence. My throat was still sore from the previous night and shouting wasn't helping either. I stepped closer to Joseph's corner and repeated my actions.

Just an eerie silence filled the lounge. My pulse was well above normal and my legs were shaking like jellies.

I heard Sam whispering my name. I turned to look at her and saw she was pointing at some seats at the opposite end of the lounge. 'There were some small lights flickering over there,' she said with a tremor in her voice.

Where Sam was pointing, I could make out the dark outline of a tall man. He was walking slowly towards me. Although he was in complete silhouette I just knew those eyes of his were glaring right at me, filled with hatred and venom. I blinked and he'd vanished!

The lounge was icy cold. He just disappeared right in front of me. I then heard an evil chuckle coming from the right-hand side of the room. There was slightly more light there. Looking in that direction I saw him lounging on a seat. He threw his head back and let out a most unholy sound of evil laughter. It sent shivers all over my body.

I walked towards him and stopped. A small table was the only thing that separated Joseph and I. He held eye contact with me as he leaned forward and spat some festering mucus from his mouth at me. The disgusting blob hit me in the chest and it's dampness immediately soaked into my top and onto my skin. I wanted to vomit and felt bile rising in my throat. I fought to keep the contents of my stomach in place. Joseph projected a thought right into my mind, 'Oh! there is much more fun I'll be having with you my sweetheart.' He laughed and slowly faded away.

I backed away and returned to the safety of the salt circle and my friends. 'I need to sit down,' was all I was able to utter. I had a thumping headache and my throat was painfully sore. I took a tissue from my bag and went to wipe Joseph's spit from my clothes. The only visible mark was a small dirty brown stain, the fabric was completely dry.

Sam was wanting to know what would be the best thing the team could do next. My suggestion was, split into two groups, one to continue digging and the other to explore more thoroughly the rooms in the pub. It was possible there could be clues that had been overlooked. Some information only I possessed, could prove very useful. The group I witnessed giving Joseph such a brutal beating, was headed by a man called George who was landlord of the Wheatsheaf. These details had been given to me whilst I had sat praying earlier. It was obvious that George held no fear of Joseph and could be instrumental in helping me release the little girl from her earthbound hell. I made a mental note to find out more about George.

Chris, Phil and Stephen volunteered to return to the storeroom and continue searching through the rubble behind the wall.

Sam and Denise wanted to join me in searching other rooms around the place. I decided to take a closer look at the ladies toilets first.

Both teams climbed the stairs together but split up when we reached the ladies toilet. The lads carried on down the corridor to the storeroom. Our small group stood at the doorway listening while I outlined what I intended to do once inside.

I went in first and created a large salt circle on the floor. I sat inside the circle and called for Sam and Denise to join me. The three of us sat quietly. I used some Reiki techniques to put myself into a relaxed state and rapidly I felt I was slipping back in time. I took note of the style and colours of the room which no longer was toilets. I tried to memorise as many details as I could.

The coldness came suddenly and I knew she was close.

22ND SEPTEMBER BREAKING NEWS

I opened my eyes to see if I could see her. There was no sign of the child but, looming up behind Sam and Denise was the shadow of a man.

'Don't move,' I whispered.

'Why?' replied Denise, her voice choked with fear.

'A man is standing right behind you and Sam,' I answered.

As the words were leaving my lips, a terrible moan reverberated right through the toilets. So loud that it hurt the eardrums and caused us to clasp hands over our ears.

Sam and Denise just screamed, stood up and ran to the toilet exit. I gathered my belongings and followed only a few paces behind them.

Standing in the corridor I managed to calm myself and the girls down. 'This is getting bad,' I said. 'You're not kidding,' retorted Sam a little less jovial than her usual self.

'She's close by Suzanne,' said Denise, 'I can feel her near.'

'Right, let's get on with it,' I said. 'The Gents is the next place to look at.'

We adopted the same procedure as the last one. I went in first while Sam and Denise stayed outside waiting for me to call.

Waiting inside for me was a spirit I recognised as Patrick, the tall thin henchman of Joseph. He gave off an evil atmosphere but was nowhere near as intimidating as Joseph. He stood blocking the way staring at me. I looked into those dead eyes and understood immediately. He was showing me scenes in the Wheatsheaf from many years ago. In a corridor downstairs appeared a slim pretty woman called Alice. She was a prostitute. She was crying. Patrick loved Alice and hated Joseph for making her work as a prostitute. The scene changed and I was looking at a very narrow corridor, so narrow that two people, couldn't pass without one stepping aside.

At the end of this corridor were three doors, the largest of which had maroon paintwork and a brass handle. I knew that I was being shown was Joseph's office. The vision changed again and I was looking directly into the office.

There was a large desk between two bay windows. The curtains and drapes were very thick and made the room look gloomy. On the desk was an ox-blood coloured leather bound book with brass trimmings. A stout wooden chair with rounded wheels standing beside the desk. The scene again changed. I was looking at the narrow corridor where a sturdily built woman called Kathleen stood. She was supervising a line of young girls who were queueing to hand money over to Joseph. I was looking at a line of prostitutes who were working for Joseph. They were giving him their takings for the day. Kathleen was looking after a brothel for Joseph!

The corridor vanished and so had Patrick. I was standing alone in the short corridor that led to the Gents. Sam and Denise had also stepped inside and were calling to me. I turned and joined them. They were full of questions about what I'd seen. I asked Sam to make some notes and she produced a writing pad and pen ready for my words.

I carefully described as much detail as I could remember whilst Sam struggled to keep up. Denise suddenly stopped me talking by saying, 'Shh!'

'What is it, Denise?' asked Sam.

'I just heard a child scream,' said Denise.

The three of us stood listening as we clearly heard another scream, then the sound of small feet running along the main corridor outside the Gents. I dashed into the corridor and looked both ways but couldn't see anything. My instincts told me to turn right and run downstairs to the lounge. On reaching the bottom step I stopped dead in my tracks. The lounge had changed. I'd been thrown back in time again. Everything was as it would have been in the early 1900's. Carpets and been replaced with worn wooden floors. There were only lanterns providing light. The walls were all painted a muddy grey colour. Standing beside the trapdoor to the cellar was Joseph. He had raised the hatch and was just stepping down onto the cellar stairs. Over his shoulder, he carried a small sack. Something was struggling within. He looked directly at me and gave me a sadistic smile. He opened the sack to reveal the little girl. She was screaming and fighting to get free but Joseph just pushed her roughly back into the sack, lowered it into the open trapdoor and followed it down into the cellar. Just as he was about to close the hatch he paused for a moment. All I could see were those evil eyes staring from the shadows, then the hatch closed.

That cruel bastard delighted in showing off his 'catch' before settling down to enjoy himself. An almighty rage exploded inside of me. I ran to the trapdoor but couldn't open it, no matter how hard I tried. I was crying and cursing and ended up sitting in a heap on the floor.

When I got my breath back I looked up to see Sam and the team standing open mouthed at the bottom of the stairs. Chris ran over to where I sat and helped get me to my feet. Everyone took their places round the table in the safe zone waiting for me to speak. It was a few minutes before I felt strong enough to answer questions.

Shirley began to tell of a haunted house they'd visited in Wales.

There was one question I needed to hear answers to first. 'Did everyone hear her screams?'

'Definitely!' said Phil!' The team all agreed with him. The screams had reached the ears of everyone present that evening.

HIDDEN EYES

'Can I ask a question Suzanne?' said Chris.

I nodded for him to ask. 'We were surprised when you ran the opposite way to the where the sounds came from, why did you do that?'.

'Do you remember the vision I had last Saturday night when I mentioned watching the girl being frightened, running down the corridor looking for someplace to hide and then going down the spiral staircase in Joseph's office?.

'Go on,' said Sam. By now everyone was intrigued.

'I realised that what we were experiencing, was a replay of that scene. I wanted to see what happened after she was captured at the bottom of the staircase.'

'And what did happen?' queried Chris.

I told them of Joseph carrying the child in a sack and taking her into the cellar. Hearing my own words describing her fate made me break down. It was all too terrible to bear.

I gained my composure and announced I was going into the cellar.

'No Suzanne!' Sam let out a gasp.

'I need to do this Sam,' I said. 'I need closure on this.'

'Ok,' she said, 'but are you up to it? I nodded.

There was a general feeling amongst the group I shouldn't do it, but nothing they said could persuade me otherwise.

'If you're sure, I'll get the cellar keys from behind the bar.'

Chris and Phil said they would finish off upstairs in the storeroom. I gave Chris a hug to thank him for all his help and understanding.

I stood by the cellar door while Sam went for the keys.

A small figure appeared in front of me. She had long brown hair, a sad little face, and was dressed in clothes typical of a child from the turn of the 20th century. She told me her name was Annabelle. She was crying for her mother because the nasty man upstairs made her wash lots of dishes in the kitchen and often beat her. I reached out to her but she just faded away.

Sam and Phil were struggling to open the main cellar hatch and when they finally got it open, the sound of cooling fans filled the air. I told Sam we'd never hear ourselves speak over the noise. Sam said she would turn the fans off, but it would only be for a short while as the cellar had to be held at a constant temperature.

Once in the cellar, the cold hit me in seconds. I placed my hand on an outside wall and began to imagine what it would have been like back in Joseph's time. I could picture horses and carriages stood in the road outside waiting for people to enter or leave the pub. What I did pick up on was, whatever dark deeds happened between these walls, remained between the walls. Joseph made sure of it. Even though George was the landlord of the Wheatsheaf, Joseph seemed to hold as much authority and sometimes even more so.

I followed the wall around to an alcove then stopped. A cold far greater and intense than the temperature created by the fans suddenly swirled about me, rooting me to the spot. I couldn't move my feet. My hands were stuck firmly by my sides.

'Get out, get out now,' I screamed. I heard scuffling as Sam and Phil dashed for the exit.

A suffocating blanket wrapped itself around me, squeezing every breath from my lungs. I prayed like I'd never prayed before in my life. I was choking. *God, please help me*. The blanket became tighter. Some invisible force was crushing me! I started to feel dizzy through lack of oxygen. A darkness was beginning to swallow me. I thought I would pass out at any moment. Bang!

All the cellar fans sprung into life at once. The shock was enough to distract whatever it was that held me. I broke free and ran out of the cellar into the open arms of Sam.

We all returned to the safe zone and sat talking about what had just happened and the pieces of a girl's shoe we had found.

Phil spoke first, 'You looked shattered Suzanne, I know tonight has been a bad one for you, but I have something more for you.' He handed over a small tin box with a man riding a penny-farthing pictured on the lid. The tin was very old and covered in dust. My heart was racing. The last time I'd seen it was when I saw the little girl putting it away into her chest of drawers.

My mind was racing. What would I find inside?, the necklace she placed there, or photographs she cherished. Carefully I lifted the lid and peered inside.

I was disappointed to find neither of those things in there.

The tin contained what appeared to be a small piece of fabric, possibly from a dress, an old matchbox branded 'Puck's' and a few wisps of what seemed to be human hair.

I just stared at the contents. There could have been more. It wasn't much but at least, it was more confirmation of the information I'd passed on.

'The tin box was found behind the wall, and we were bringing it along to show you when an icy cold breeze swept past us in the corridor. Next thing, you shot out of the Gents and went running downstairs,' said Phil. Tired eyes looked at the tin.

We were all too worn out to talk anymore.

The night had come and gone. Another day was pushing the night out of the sky and everyone present was ready for bed. We quickly arranged one more night for a search and went our separate ways.

Once in the car park, something made me look up at the building. There, at the window facing the car park, was the little girl. She only appeared for a fleeting moment but I swear, she had the beginnings of a smile on her tear-stained little face.

23rd September
Second Opinion

I laid thinking about all the situations I had faced during the previous few days.

Many things had happened in such a short time. As one event ended another more gruelling one took its place. Just when I thought everything was making sense, a new piece of the jigsaw appeared and changed my way of thinking.

My life was in turmoil.

Mark had been right about one thing, I'd allowed the Wheatsheaf to take over my life. Too many hours had been spent there. I'd become obsessed with the child and I couldn't fully understand why. Yes, I felt strongly about her predicament and wished to get her away from Joseph, but something else was gnawing at the edges of my instinct.

It was like looking at something behind frosted glass. You could make out something was there but the shape wasn't clear enough to identify with certainty. It was definitely something connected with Joseph and the child. But what?

I was getting a better picture of what Joseph had been up to. From what I'd seen, it appeared he was nothing more than a pimp, working from an office in the pub itself. He could have only done that with the permission of the

Landlord George who, no doubt, was getting his pockets well lined for his troubles. Joseph, with the help of Kathleen, ruled his workforce with violence and threats, keeping them prisoner in the upstairs rooms or in the house next door. Any girl who bucked the system was quietly disposed of, along with any young ones, unless they could serve a useful purpose.

Joseph must have been making a fortune. Maybe that's how he was able to live in the Mansion House!

I still couldn't figure out the significance of the little girl or why Joseph seemed hell bent on stopping me connecting with her. I thought it was because he wanted her for himself, to have her dwell in his ungodly realm forever. Maybe I would find out. Maybe I wouldn't, but I wasn't going to give in without a fight.

I felt a tear roll down my cheek as I thought about all the poor souls who'd passed through the clutches of Joseph.

Lives ruined with imprisonment and prostitution. No escape and no hope. Children forced into slavery and their mothers discarded like worthless rubbish once their earnings failed to satisfy him.

Then there was my home life.

Things between Mark and I were at an all time low. We barely spoke anymore, just enough to get by and manage the day to day domestic side of things. There were occasional moments of closeness but it was safe to say we'd past the stage of love's first bloom.

The children were another worry. I felt the closeness Francesca and I shared was suffering from recent events. I was noticing that she had started to turn to Mark for certain things, when in the past it, had always been me. Alex, due his age, was less of a problem. Provided he was fed regularly, it didn't matter who held the spoon. I could feel myself changing, but was it going to be beneficial to my family?

My friendship with Sam, Denise, Chris and Phil also troubled me.

What on earth had I dragged those decent people into? Every time I turned up at the Wheatsheaf, it seemed to cause them at the least headaches, but too many times, moments of danger too. I reflected upon the painfully long sessions we spent digging away upstairs, based solely on my belief. Their lives had been disrupted just as much as mine had, but I'd never heard one of them question what I was doing. Their loyalty and belief in me was very special. I couldn't have done it without them.

Alex's crying was enough to break my thoughts and bring me back to reality. I had a house party booked in for the afternoon. Checking the time I saw it was less than two hours away. I really felt inclined to cancel but, that was one thing I tried to avoid at all costs. In my business reliability is essential.

Putting those thoughts aside, I gave my attention to Alex and he quickly stopped crying. Mark came into the lounge and said sarcastically, I wondered how long he was going to keep crying until you noticed him!' 'Aw, get lost Mark will you?' I bit back, and immediately regretted it. I needed him to look after Alex and collect Fran from school while I went to the house party.

I apologised and he forgave me after a bit of moaning. I sweetened the babysitting request by adding, if I made enough, I would bring him some beers in. That seemed to do the trick. We shared out the housework between us and for a while, we were back to business as usual.

I was upstairs cleaning the bathroom when I heard my mobile ringing downstairs. By the time I entered the lounge, Mark had answered the call for me. He thrust the phone towards me saying, 'It's one of your mates from that pub.' I took it from him and said, 'Hi, Suzanne Gill,'. The voice at the other end of the line said, 'Hi Suzanne,' and I recognised it as Denise.

'Hi Suzanne, I'll keep it brief because Mark said you were going out soon.'

'Ok,' I replied, curious to the reason for her call.

'I've been thinking about what you have been going through at the pub. I reckon I might have come up with a suggestion that could help you,' she said.

Denise now had my full attention. 'Go on then, what?'.

'I think you need a second opinion from another medium.' she said.

It was a simple statement, but one I hadn't thought of.

Ping! A light in my head just lit up. I was trying to make sense of too much by myself! Another psychic could possibly see things that I'd missed. 'That's brilliant,' I said.

'There's a couple from Durham who are supposed to be amazing, he's called Simon and his wife is called Shirley. Do you want me try and make some arrangements for tonight?' she suggested.

'That would be great Densie. Thanks. I'll see you at the pub,' I said, before hanging up.

I was now up against the clock. I had just enough time to get ready and get to the house party, but any traffic delays and I would be late.

I got ready in record time and flew from the house after saying goodbye to Mark and Alex.

Driving to the house party I thought about the conversation I'd just had with Denise.

I loved the idea of a second opinion. What a brilliant suggestion. I thought it was definitely the best course of action to take.

I drove to the estate where my satnav was directing me.

HIDDEN EYES

I arrived at a biggish house with a long winding driveway. I could see a lady standing at the window waving as she saw my car driving onto her property.

I parked and was greeted by a lovely young girl who came out of the house to meet me at the end of the driveway. She thanked me for coming and walked me up to the house.

In the hallway, I noticed it was a warm cream colour and I could make out the smell of fresh paint. It felt like a breath of fresh air to be in such light and bright surroundings after spending so much time in the dark and dismal Wheatsheaf.

I could hear laughter coming from the room to my right, a group of women were in there happily enjoying themselves.

A lady I estimated to be in her forties, stepped into the hallway and introduced herself as the host, Tracey and the young girl stood beside me as her daughter Louise.

Tracey ushered me into the living room and I was met by six very enthusiastic women, eager for their personal readings. I was given a lovely warm welcome. Tracey told me she'd set up her conservatory as my reading area. It had a nice atmosphere and I thought it was just right for me. There was a small glass table in the centre of the room decorated with two large bunches of assorted flowers and tea lights. The fragrance from the flowers was beautiful and filled the conservatory without being too overpowering. Louise took it upon herself to look after me whilst I was a guest there. I was given a pot of tea and a plate of delicious biscuits

After each reading, Louise came into the conservatory to ask if everything was alright and checked if I needed any more tea or biscuits.

The afternoon passed quickly, and each lady I sat with

seemed very pleased with their reading. I finished off by reading for Louise and finally her mother Tracey. Both mother and daughter came to the front door to wave as I set off for home. What a lovely afternoon it had been. So different to the last week I'd endured.

It was almost teatime, where had the day gone to? I wondered.

During the drive home, I noticed a tightness in my chest, and that raw sort of feeling when a cold is starting. *That's all I need. I haven't time to be ill* I said to myself. Maybe the many hours spent in freezing cold rooms breathing in cement dust was to blame.

By the time I got home, the tightness in my chest had developed into a cough. I was getting a temperature, and my throat was feeling raw.

I somehow managed to drag myself out of the car and into the house, only to be met by Francesca jumping up and down as I came through the front door. She was excitedly telling me about the rehearsals the school had held for the Christmas nativity play. I gave her some encouraging words but the cold symptoms were preventing me from being ecstatic.

Mark was sat in the lounge watching TV while Alex was crawling around on the floor beside him. The place looked like a tip. 'You could have tidied up a bit,' I said in an annoyed voice to Mark. He didn't react, so I grabbed the remote and turned the tv off.

'Hey!' he shouted, 'I was watching that.'

I was in no mood to take the argument any further so I set about picking up all the clutter lying around the room.

Mark just turned the TV back on and continued watching it.

Once I'd got the place looking reasonable, I turned my attention to Alex.

HIDDEN EYES

I crept up on him and went 'Boo,' he started giggling and I joined in on his laughter. Fran must have heard us, because she came down from her room to see what was funny. Mark in the meantime stood up and left the room. Fran had a good connection with her baby brother and quickly took over, allowing me to go and find Mark.

I found him in the dining room. 'Can we talk?' I asked.

'If you must,' he replied.

'Sorry I snapped earlier,' I said.

'Look, Suzanne, it's not just you. I don't know what's happening to us, or where this will end up, but I know we can't go on like this. We're making each other miserable.'

If I was totally honest with myself I'd have to admit, he was right. Still there was more than just me and Mark to think about. What about Fran and Alex. Would it be more damaging for them to have parents that were constantly arguing or a single mum trying to cope with two children and be self-employed?

It wasn't the right time to figure that one out, as I was feeling the full effects of a chest infection.

Mark gave me a sort of smile, nodded and said, 'Ok, shall I get you some flu tablets and a glass of water?' I accepted his offer and was soon swallowing what I hoped was a remedy that would make me feel better.

I went to pick Alex up but as I bent over I started coughing. At first, I tried to stifle it, but I just stood there getting red in the face, the cough grew worse. Mark came over to me and tried patting me on the back. That helped a little, then he went and got me a glass of water. I felt much better after that.

Francesca looked worried, but a few words and a quick cuddle put her mind at rest. After several minutes had passed I was a different person. I was well enough to prepare the tea for all of us and we sat as a family enjoying

23^(RD) SEPTEMBER SECOND OPINION

a tasty pizza and salad.

We sat watching one of Fran's favourite videos, 'Finding Nemo', it was fortunate that Alex enjoyed all the colours in it otherwise I think he would have started wailing.

At the end of the film, I told Fran it was time for bed so she gave me a hug and kiss then skipped off upstairs. She shouted 'Goodnight,' as she left the room. 'Goodnight babe,' I called after her.

'Are you going over to Boldon tonight?' asked Mark.

'I am supposed to meet up with Sam and the rest about 10 pm,' I told him.

'I don't think you're up to it, you've started wheezing like an old carthorse,' said Mark.

'But I have no choice, in an ideal world, I should be taking a few days off to let this flu work itself out of my system. I also realised that it could get a lot worse over the next week. I want to take my chances and go tonight,' I told him.

I fully expected us to end up in a blazing row but no, he just shrugged his shoulders and said softly, 'Ok but be careful, and remember to take your flu tablets with you.'

Even getting dressed to go out was an effort but I made sure I layered up well to withstand the Wheatsheaf coldness. I had very mixed feelings about what lay ahead. What would I be told by the mediums I was going to meet? Would we find anything more in the storeroom search?

With half an hour before the meeting due in the Wheatsheaf at 10 pm I walked to the front door. Mark helped me on with my coat and I picked up my bag.

'Remember to give me a call will you,' he said and we hugged briefly before I left.

I was coughing and spluttering as I climbed into the car. The cold air must have got onto my chest. I had to sit for a couple of minutes until everything settled down before I was able to drive.

It didn't take long to get to the Wheatsheaf from where I lived and I was soon pulling up at the place like I had done so many times over the last few days. I think the car could have found its own way there.

The lounge was empty so I made my way through to the bar. There were several people in. I recognized a few faces and they waved or nodded when seeing me. I smiled back and went to the bar counter. Julie the barmaid, a slim blonde girl was being kept busy with the serious drinkers. I'd spoken to her only a couple of times, but she immediately recognised me as I stood waiting to be served.

'Hi Suzanne,' she said with a smile. 'What can I get you?'

I asked for a soft drink so I could take some flu tablets. My throat was starting to hurt again.

I cast my eyes over the people who were there. The usual crowd were in plus a couple of old guys playing dominoes and a gang of lads round the pool table. However, I noticed a tall heavy built man sitting at the far end of the bar, he stood out a mile from everyone else. My instincts told me, he was the medium Simon, who'd been arranged by Denise, and the one I was supposed to be meeting that evening. He was well turned out, I estimated his age to be about sixty and had the look of an intelligent man with a distinguished air about him. Alongside him sat a grey-haired woman who looked slightly older. She was smartly dressed and looked a little out of place in the bar of the Wheatsheaf.

I looked at the couple sitting there and hopes were starting to build up inside me. *Please let them identify something that I've overlooked. Just one thing to give the little girl the peace she needs, would be enough.*

23RD SEPTEMBER SECOND OPINION

My thoughts were interrupted when Julie placed my drink on the counter and said, 'There you go Suzanne, and here's your change.'

I picked up the change and my drink, then walked over to where the couple sat. Simon stood up as I approached the table.

'Hi, Suzanne Gill,' I said offering to shake hands with him. 'Simon James and this is my wife Shirley'. Shirley remained sitting but did lean forward to also shake my hand. Simon had a deep Durham sounding accent. Shirley had no noticeable accent whatsoever.

'Do you mind if I join you?' I asked.

'Not all, please sit with us,' Shirley said extending her welcome to me.

'So you are the mediums that I hope can help me,' I said.

'We'll do our best, but first can you give us some background as to what's been happening, and why you need us to get involved,' said Simon.

I gave them a brief rundown on the basic details. Various expressions, from amazement to sadness, passed over their faces as details were described.

They sat silently for a minute or so before Simon spoke first.

'That's some problem you have Suzanne', he said. 'I hope we can live up to your expectations.'

Shirley leaned across the table, took a hold of my hand and said, 'We'll do everything we can love. I can see how much it means to you. We're on your side. I know the staff here have been helping, but all the psychic matters you've been taking on by yourself. There's no need to feel you are fighting this alone anymore.'

Those words were like music to my ears. I felt overwhelmed at what I'd just heard. The 'Thank you' I gave them, in no way gave them any idea of the enormous relief that filled me.

We started to talk about other topics and I wanted to ask about the silver angel necklace set with a purple amethyst that Shirley was wearing. It captivated me the way the light glistened in the stone.

'Shirley, can I ask, where did you get that beautiful necklace?'

'Oh this,' she replied, holding the necklace between her thumb and index finger, 'it's from Dubai; we had it specially made for the type of work Simon and I do.'

'Wow! Tell me more,' I said intrigued to hear more about their experiences.

'Well,' said Simon smiling at Shirley sitting to his left, we are what you could call, demonologists, specialising in psychic investigation and spiritual cleansing. Although we live in Sedgefield, we travel around, helping traumatized people who are suffering the effects of evil spirits.'

'Oh My God,' I said wanting to hear more. It had been an ambition of mine for years to get into their line of work.

I suggested that we took our drinks into the lounge where it was quieter. The lads round the pool table were getting a bit excited over their match, and it was becoming slightly more difficult to have a comfortable conversation.

We grabbed our drinks and I led the way into the lounge. I chose the safe area. We more or else sat in the same positions we'd had in the bar with me with my back to the room and the couple facing me.

Shirley began to tell of a haunted house they'd visited in Wales. 'Oh yes,' she smiled I could see her expression change as she recalled the things that had happened there. I listened intently, drawn in by the verbal picture she was painting. Shirley was an incredible narrator. Her story involved the spirit of a nine-year-old boy that was causing a great deal of distress to the family who lived in the property. Objects were being moved, ornaments fell from shelves when nobody was near them, and bedclothes were sometimes dragged off the sleeping occupants.

As Shirley was about to continue her intriguing story, I noticed from the corner of my eye, Simon was sitting bolt upright and staring over my shoulder towards Joseph's corner. He had a totally blank look on his face. He stood suddenly with arms just hanging at his side. The whites of his eye were showing and his mouth was open slightly. His breathing was quite laboured and I reached over to touch his arm.

'Don't,' whispered Shirley, 'leave him be, he's gone into a trance.' She gently took his arm and pulled him down into a sitting position. He stayed in the same strange state as he sat down.

Taking Simon's left hand she turned to me and said, 'Try and remember the things he mentions. I will hold his hand to help with the communication.'

My pulse started to race. It was the first time I'd seen a trance medium working. I didn't know what to expect. Was I about to find out the information that had become my quest over the past week?

I waited. There was a deadly silence in the lounge. Simon sat totally expressionless.

Suddenly his head turned towards me.

'Joseph wants YOU,' said Simon darkly.

His voice had taken on a snarling sound and he was bearing his teeth. 'He wants you to feel pain. He wants to possess you. He wants you to pay for your interfering and meddling. For stepping into his domain. For trying to connect with the child.'

Simon's voice became dry and hoarse.

His face seemed to change into a sort of mask that

looked like Joseph.

'Stop now or I will make you take your own life,' said the voice that came from Simon's mouth. A voice I was very familiar with.

Simon slumped forward onto the table. Shirley gave a little cry and tried to lift his shoulders. I sat frozen to the spot.

'Suzanne, help me,' shouted Shirley. That was enough to snap me out of my state of fear. I joined her in lifting Simon off the table and into an upright position. He sat blinking and rubbing his eyes.

Simon looked at me as I sat back down opposite him and said in a soft voice, 'Would you like to give us the full story now? We've already had the bare bones. Now put some meat on them.'

They got what they asked for. Every twist and turn. Remembering it brought tears back to my eyes, the tears became sobs and I ended up crying like a baby in front of them. They allowed me time to recover before speaking.

'I'm confused. Did I get this right? You had never been here before last week?' asked Simon with a puzzled look on his face.

'I first walked into this place on the 15th of this month, why, what's the matter?' I replied.

He turned to Shirley who was still holding his hand and said, 'The matter is,' he paused before turning back to me, 'You have been connected with this place for a very long time young lady.'

'How?' I asked.

'You have had a previous life here,' he replied.

This was all too much for me to take in. My head was spinning.

23rd September
Lifting The Blindfold

Shirley came over and helped me stand. My legs were shaking and I felt as weak as a kitten.

'You are looking quite pale Suzanne, I think you should splash some water on your face, and if you're going to the loo, I think I'll pay a visit as well,' she said in a disguised way of keeping an eye on me.

We walked slowly up the stairs and along the corridor to the ladies toilets. We didn't exchange any words on the way there, which was highly unusual in the normal run of things. On entry, I went to the mirror above the hand basin. I looked awful. Tired and drawn with mascara all over my face. Similar to a weird looking panda.

I could see Shirley's reflection in the mirror as she stood behind me. She had a sympathetic look on her face.

'You've been through it love, haven't you?' she said.

'Don't Shirley, or you'll start me off crying again and I've just fixed my eyes,' I protested.

She paced around the room and then stopped and asked, 'Does this room have any significance to you Suzanne?'

'Yes,' I replied, 'This room used to be the little girl's bedroom and I believe it holds the key to what happened here, all those years ago.'

HIDDEN EYES

'Interesting...' she said, walking over to the sink to wash her hands. We made our way from the toilets and back onto the landing. I couldn't help but notice that Shirley was paying close attention to details as we walked back down the stairs.

As we neared the bottom of the stairs I heard the distinctive squeal of Sam's laughter. A small crowd had gathered in the lounge. 'Before we join the others I want to say something,' said Shirley. She turned to me and said, 'Please don't mention to anybody what my husband told you. I asked her 'why?' and she replied, 'The message Simon gave you was a personal one. Not for sharing.' Her request in a weird way somehow made sense to me.

As we stepped into the lounge, Shirley left my side and went to sit beside her husband. Sam spotted me and shrieked, 'Suzanne!', then ran over to give me a big hug. We walked to the counter and Sam tapped on the bar to get Julie's attention. Julie was serving in the Bar and didn't hear Sam. Because there was no instant response, Sam placed her handbag on the counter and said, 'Oh for God's sake, if you want a job doing properly, then do it yourself.'. With that, she went behind the bar to take matters into her own hands.

'What are you having Suzanne? it's on me.'

'I'll have a glass of water if you don't mind Sam?' I answered.

'Water, you're kidding aren't you?' she responded.

'Sorry, Sam but I've got this raging flu or something coming on, and I'm taking tablets.'

'Ok, fair enough,' was Sam's reply.

I'd managed to keep clear of another coughing fit for several hours, maybe it wouldn't develop into anything worse, but to be on the safe side, I took 2 more tablets, just in case.

23RD SEPTEMBER LIFTING THE BLINDFOLD

Denise came and stood beside me as Sam continued serving drinks.

'Is that the mediums over there?' she said pointing towards Simon and Shirley.

'I thought you knew them, Denise?'

'Sorry if I gave you that impression Suzanne. I knew of them through the Spiritualist Churches I go to, they're supposed to be brilliant, but I've never seen them myself,' she replied.

'Well we've met already tonight and they're a lovely couple. You've done me proud Denise. You couldn't have picked anyone better. Thank you,' I said showing my appreciation for her good judgement.

I felt that Simon and Shirley had spent too long sitting by themselves and it was about time they should meet the members of the team who'd arrived.

Beckoning the group over, I proceeded to carry out introductions and suggested we all sat together.

One of the first introductions was Denise to Simon.

'So you are the lady responsible for us being here tonight?' he said shaking Denise's hand.

She smiled at him and admitted she was.

I asked Shirley what she and Simon had planned for the evening.

'Well,' said Shirley, 'is everyone here who is taking part in tonight's get together?'

Sam told her there were two more to come.

'Then that is a problem. It makes the number of people too high for us to work with,' replied Shirley as she continued 'At any sitting we hold there had to be seven people around the table.'

Denise's son Stephen chipped in and said, 'Look I'll drop out if that helps. I was only coming along to make up the numbers. To be honest I'd rather go and have a game of pool. If somebody doesn't turn up, give me a shout and I'll come back in.'

Denise said, 'Thanks son, that does help.'

I could understand what Shirley was saying, that's their way of working with trance mediumship. Everyone has their own way of working and this was obviously hers. I could see Denise was looking at me, she was trying to draw my attention. She was sitting next to Sam on the seats opposite me, so I swapped seats and sat next to Sam.

'So what do you think of the mediums?' Denise was sitting at the table, her camera placed on her lap.

'Yes... I like Shirley, she is lovely, but Simon doesn't say much does he?'

'Well, we can only wait and see,' I replied.

'Sam said they better be good because it was costing us £45 for their services.'

'What?' I said, looking over to the couple. 'I thought they were doing this as volunteers like me.' 'No,' said Denise as she shook her head, 'they asked if we all would put some money in for their costs.'

I was thinking to myself that it had been worth £45. 00 for the information that Simon had told me about Joseph earlier, that alone was priceless. It was just what I needed to hear, he had confirmed some information to me already and although it was upsetting, it had made me sure that I was on the right path.

As the bottom door slammed shut, I could see Chris and Phil walking towards us, I was glad to see they'd arrived. This meant we could now carry on with the mediumship session. Chris gave a cheery welcome as he came over to where Sam and I were sitting.

'Hi, you lot,' he said with a smile, I noticed he had a bag under his arm with writings and books for me to have a look at later that night, he said he had been to the library earlier on that day and that he had some more interesting information about Joseph.

Wow! I thought, feeling impressed by how determined Chris was to help find this little girl.

'Right,' I said to Sam, 'are we going to get the wheels into motion, I really want to find out what our guests discover upstairs.'

'Yes,' came the replies from Sam and Denise. 'We are ready to go.' I looked towards Simon and Shirley and smiled.

'Are you both ready to make a start?' I asked.

'Oh yes,' said Shirley as she stood up, her husband Simon followed close behind her. They went to the bottom of the stairs and waited for me and the rest of the group to lead the way.

At the top of the landing next to the ladies' toilets, I felt a cold shiver run up and down my spine. From experience, I knew that this was Joseph's way of letting me know he was close by. He was watching my every move. Simon stopped at the top of the landing. He was looking around in all directions. I stepped back to give him some space. He looked at me and pointed to the ladies' toilets saying, 'I feel there has been a tragedy here in this area,' his breathing was becoming deeper. I asked if he was picking up on any more information about what had happened. 'NO 'he said and shook his head. He asked me to lead him through the other rooms. I took him along the corridor to the Gents and was about to open the door when Simon placed his hand on my shoulder.

He stepped back and pointed to the door, 'I don't feel anything in that room. Can you show me the room you have been digging in; I see bricks on the floor.' I asked Sam for the keys to the door at the end of the corridor that led to the two rooms beyond.

'Here you go Suzanne,' said Sam, handing me the keys. I was nervous wondering what Simon was going to discover. As I opened the door we were greeted with an icy cold breeze that rushed into the corridor. I found the switch and turned on the light. A shiver shot down my spine. I took hold of the storeroom door handle and immediately I realized it was icy cold. It took some force to push open the door. I let out a gasp as icy cold air and dust combined hit the back of my throat and left me gasping for breath.

'Are you okay?' asked Simon putting his arm around my waist to stop me falling over. All I could do at that moment was manage a nod.

He walked me over to the seat beside the window. I began to gag. The smell of the dust was nauseating. I didn't want to be in that room.

Sam offered me some reassurance, 'Take it easy Suzanne, let me know if your breathing gets any worse, and I'll take you downstairs.'

'Thanks Sam,' I replied.

The group were standing together in the centre of the room. Shirley began to provide some details of what was going to happen and what was required.

'We need seven chairs set out in a circle here, and a small table standing in the centre.'

Phil and Chris volunteered to fetch some chairs and left the room.

Simon was walking slowly round the room not engaging in any contact with the group. He tilted his head as if listening to something then took a few more steps. He examined the walls, placing his hand flat on the embossed paper. The chimney breast held his interest for a minute or two. Then he looked into the gaping hole we'd created over the past few days, paused, took a step back and bowed very slightly from the waist. It was such a subtle movement I don't think anyone there noticed but me. He had never been told what we'd hope to find behind that wall. All he knew was we were searching for clues. That small gesture of Simon's was like a sign from heaven. It captured and portrayed everything I'd hoped for simultaneously. He came and stood beside me.

'I know you are looking for answers in this room,' he said solemnly. 'But you must also understand the grave danger you could find yourself in. He is watching you. Watching and waiting for the right moment to take you. You must protect yourself and ask your guides to give you strength.'

This stark warning struck home. It was like getting hit with an iron rod. I was feeling dizzy. Whether it was the words Simon had just spoken or the chest infection I couldn't be sure but it didn't matter. All I knew was, my physical condition wasn't great, just when I needed it most.

Phil and Chris by now had seven chairs and a small table set up in a circle as requested by Shirley.

Simon took his seat as head of the circle. I sat at his right side, Shirley's seat was to his left. Denise was on my right then Sam Chris and Phil took the remaining seats.

Before she sat down Shirley created a circle of salt around the outside of our chairs. As she did so I could hear her softly reciting some words of a prayer. She then lit a candle that stood inside a small red glass lantern. Simon informed the group that spirits were attracted to red light and could become visible in that part of the spectrum. The soft red glow gave off just enough light to see each other but darkness obscured all the detail outside the circle.

'Are we all ready?' asked Shirley and a number of uncertain voices replied, 'Yes.'

Simon sat very upright with his hands resting lightly on his thighs. Shirley went and stood behind him, placing her hands on his shoulders. She had her eyes closed.

Several minutes passed, nothing seemed to be happening. I checked everyone sitting in the circle and saw Sam was also looking around. The only sound was Simon's breathing becoming slower and louder. I could see Shirley's breathing was matching that of Simon. The light from the red lantern seemed to be going dimmer then brighter and the flame started flickering.

A coldness was swirling around the room as the seven of us sat motionless. I felt something gripping my hand. My heart missed several beats. I looked down and saw that Simon had taken my hand in his. Shirley must have been watching for this because she immediately told everyone to join hands. Once satisfied her instruction was being carried out, she took her seat next to Simon and completed the circle.

More time passed and Simon's breathing was so shallow I thought he had stopped. I could tell he was going deeper and deeper into a trance. Even Shirley looked as if she'd drifted into a dreamlike state.

Simon's face started to take on a strange look. His face was changing and becoming distorted. He was looking younger and stronger. More powerful. Sounds started to form in his throat. Gutteral sounds almost like grunting, like somebody learning to speak again after many years of silence.

Eventually, the sounds became recognizable as words.

'The child you seek is here. She has waited so long for you. The pain of separation has been unbearable for her. She is in your blood. You and her are one.'

A slow moving cloud was starting to tumble from the hole in the chimney breast wall. It slid down the wall and began to gently circulate around the perimeter of the chairs. The temperature in the room dropped even further and I could feel an icy breeze gripping my chest as I tried to breathe some air into my lungs.

I couldn't take in what was being said. Until a week ago, I never knew this little spirit even existed.

Simon continued, 'She has stood for many years looking from the window, waiting for you to come for her.

My feet were getting colder. I looked down at them and was stunned to see the cloud was beginning to pool around my ankles. Wispy tendrils were inching their way up my legs.

I looked around me. I was unable to move a muscle. I saw the faces of my friends etched in horror, at what they witnessing.

Seeing those expressions filled me with as much fear as the strange sensations I was starting to notice.

An ice cold pressure was pressing down against my upper body. It was suffocating. A cold dampness was spreading up my neck and onto my face. I was being overwhelmed by the cloud which now covered me from head to foot.

Wisps of the cloud danced before my eyes making me lose all sense of orientation. I couldn't tell if I were standing or sitting, which way was the floor, and which way was the ceiling.

The cloud started to enter my ears, nostrils and mouth.

I was breathing it in.

I prepared myself for a terrible reaction I would have when the coldness hit my lungs.

It never came.

Instead, a beautiful serene warmth was spreading into all parts of my body. A spiritual ecstasy filled my body.

The rawness in my lungs had gone. I was no longer shivering despite the coldness elsewhere in the room.

Another part of me, one that had been missing all my

life and never knew existed, had come home.

The child whose name I now held in my heart was called Jessica. We had been reunited. She was free at last.

The blindfold had been lifted and I could see the truth.

Her spirit had merged with me. We'd become one again, just like we always had been. We were the same being!

Suddenly small lights started appearing in the air above the circle.

We all sat gazing at them as each tiny orb took it in turn to brush the side of my face before rising up towards the ceiling. I could hear faint voices whispering, 'Thank you,' and 'Goodbye,' as their brightness diminished.

Witnessing those lost souls finding release was one of the most wonderful and rewarding experiences I'd ever had.

Simon gasped loudly and slumped forward in his chair. Shirley quickly left her chair and began attending to her husband.

We all let go of each others hands and an incredible feeling of positivity reached everyone within the circle.

We had all been on an incredible journey without leaving our chairs.

Shirley was the first to speak, 'I think we should all go downstairs and get warmed through. Simon is clearly exhausted and he should sit for a while to recover before we go on our way.'

Sam and Chris said they would go ahead and make sure a warming brew would be waiting for us.

Simon was fully conscious and took hold of my hand.

'I hope that's what you wanted Suzanne?' he smiled.

I put an arm round his neck and held him close.

'We are together again,' I whispered into his ear.

He just nodded and left the room with Shirley.

Denise and I were the last to leave. As we walked down the stairs together, I told her how grateful I was to her for arranging the evening.

We all sat drinking tea and chatting pleasantly together. There was plenty of questions fired in my direction about the séance. It's quite easy to forget that most of what I see, isn't what others see.

It became apparent everyone saw the white cloud and the orbs, but almost everything else remained unseen except to Simon and myself.

We all said our farewells and shook hands.

I was becoming tearful. So much had been shared with these lovely people and they would now always be a part of my life.

I blinked as the early morning sunshine hurt my eyes after the gloom inside the Wheatsheaf.

It had all started just a few days ago when I'd parked my car here for the first time.

I looked up at the small window above the side entrance where I remembered first seeing Jessica.

A movement caught my eye, then Joseph appeared, his face in a twisted rage. He was looking down at me. I stared at him and thought to myself, 'You're rid of him now!'

I turned to get into my car and managed a little smile.

Suddenly a voice pushed its way forcibly into my thoughts.

'This is not over!' growled Joseph.

To Be Continued

Made in the USA
Charleston, SC
19 April 2016